The City of Hay'at
A Collection of Seemingly Unrelated Stories

The City of Hay'at

A Collection of Seemingly Unrelated Stories

Kasra B. Fard

To my gals: Noushin and Nika

Treasure Map

The city of Hay'at is located behind an impenetrable wall of trees.

Part 1

The City of Hay'at

1—Dr. Burgess

True free-spirited travelers never deliberately plan for their thrilling journeys. These people, guided either by the desire for solitude or by the yearning for a distant chance of making an unexpected discovery, disregard the social convention that no matter how tiresome, mundane, and boring ordinary lives are, people are not to set out to bring color and enjoyment to their dreary lives, for people long for stability and distrust change.

Such travelers take no notice of the notion that the dull routine of everyday life is the integral part of human heritage that no one should do without. These travelers, therefore, are always ready to deconstruct the structure of their ordinary lives; making an unexpected discovery, however, would be an amazing bonus. Many do not even expect to achieve such a bonus; the journey is the reward, they will tell themselves, their relatives, and their friends.

In this day and age, hardly anyone would expect to make any new discovery in any field. It is widely known that physical science is the foundation of all sciences, and it was reported a few years ago that while it is never safe to say that the future of physical science has no opportunities for further growth, most of the underlying principles have already been discovered and established.[1] Therefore, there would not be any value in trying to discover or establish

---

[1] Albert Michelson, *Light Waves and Their Uses* (Chicago: The University of Chicago Press, 1903), 23–24.

new ones. By definition, we are at the point in history that we have discovered all that there is. A groundbreaking report like this one, coming from a well-established university, would surely discourage any would-be discoverer. We live in a stable world. We have explored sky, land, and sea. Yet hardened travelers remain hopeful.

Being spontaneous, these travelers might decide on starting their journeys from any part of the world. Some—for reasons beyond anybody's understanding—might decide to start off in the Andes Mountains. Regardless of where their starting points are, they do know that taking a deep, refreshing breath is the first step of any journey.

Let us follow in the footsteps of such a traveler, one who starts off from the Andes Mountains to break the mundanity of his life. Having taken a deep breath, our traveler will be ready to jump off one of the mountains right into the Ucayali River, which originates from the Andes and will later become one of the major headstreams of the Amazon River.

Our traveler will set off on his journey. We have not yet disclosed the identity of the traveler. For now, and only for simplicity, we use the masculine pronoun to identify *him*. Swimming for exactly 908.5 miles in the Ucayali River, our courageous traveler will find himself in the middle of the 208th largest and the 104th most attractive marsh in South America.

This marsh, being as old as time, marks the end of the Ucayali River and the beginning of the town of Nauta. One needs to be extra careful before entering the marsh, as this is where the Ucayali joins the Marañón River. Looking to the right and then the left before entering the marsh is compulsory since those who, on their quest, have chosen to swim the Marañón River will eventually end up in this marsh as well. Collisions would be deadly.

The survival of any traveler depends on his or her familiarity with the first law of life: to share. Our traveler is no exception. He will need to be a sharing person, or tremendous hazards will await him, especially at this juncture of his journey.

After sharing, patience is the next law of life that he will have to exercise here until he finds an empty spot to flop out of the river and into the marsh. The natural beauty of the marsh and the delta can entice anyone to end his or her quest and settle down right there. Even an iron-willed man or woman of God, vowed not to be inveigled by any earthly feeling, is no exception. This is the place where our traveler can see the remains of various camps, which other travelers before him put up when they could not demonstrate adequate willpower and determination to continue their journeys beyond this heavenly ground.

If, however, our voyager can show sufficient determination, he might be able to muster up the will to continue on his route and soon leave the marsh. The reward for tapping into the finite amount of willpower that one has will be the opportunity to visit the most gorgeous daughter of Mother Nature, the Amazon.

Once upon a time, there was a region extending from the mouth of the Danube River on the Black Sea to the east of the Aral Sea, occupied by a powerful and wise nation: the great and ancient nation of Scythia.

The last survivor of the great nation of Scythia, Ms. Amazon, punished by Zeus for disobeying him, was sentenced to relinquish her legitimate right to own a secure place to rest her soul upon. Having received the ruling, she was ordered to leave her land, Eurasia. She chose to move to the land of opportunities, South America, where her indefatigable soul floats from the Andes to the Atlantic and flies back from the Atlantic to the Andes until the end of time. Ironically, what any being regards as Amazon's essence of beauty is in reality her punishment.

The exile, conversely, never changed her nature. As always, she is as fiery as she is beautiful; moreover, she is a fearless warrior whose sly nature hides her true temperament long enough to let a naïve traveler be deceived and enter her womb, where the most horrifying of consequences await him.

The riverbank, as a matter of fact, is only a bog. It is written that by taking the mud-covered road on the right side of the bog, one could be en route to the forest of the dead—that is, if one is determined enough to step one's right foot in front of one's left foot and then the left foot in front of the right 208,104 times.

Some people live under the illusion that the Amazonian jungles are becoming more docile nowadays; this, however, is utterly wrong. The jungles, although becoming weak, are still as majestic as they are deadly. For centuries, explorers have been trying to tame the aggressive Amazonian essence.

Exploring the Amazonian jungles is not an easy task; one must prepare oneself for the fact that, although there are many roads, driving deep inside the dark, foggy habitat of grisons is quite impossible. Flying through the intertwined trees is not an option either. Walking is the only means of moving around if one is determined to reach the forest of the dead. The forest of the dead is the last explored part of the jungles. The forest is where the sight of the rising sun glinting on the trees can be seen for the last time before the surroundings all of a sudden turn pitch black. What lies beyond the forest of the dead is still a mystery; very few have ever walked farther than this forest. It is not farfetched to assume that those who managed did so with the help of Virgil. At any rate, they never came back to teach others how they managed and to tell others the stories of the appealing adventures that wait ahead. If a traveler truly intends to discover something new or see a place no one else has seen, the forest of the dead is surely where to start.

Providing that our traveler anticipates the troubles ahead in his undertaking and understands the importance of precise planning and the foresight of military operation, he might manage to reach the forest of the dead even without the help of Virgil. In this forsaken part of the world, there is no sound of any child crying, there are no sounds of people hunting or cooking — only the fizzling of snakes and the twittering of avifauna.

Now it is time for us to reveal the identity of our traveler, one of the few men who ever managed to set foot beyond the forest of the dead: the determined and famous Dr. J. Burgess. Dr. J., the most respected anthropologist and explorer of his time, needs no introduction. His explorations, discoveries, and books have been the topics of the most prestigious scientific discussions for thousands of days. His last expedition received much publicity as well. He could not manage to persuade other scientists to accompany him on this incredible expedition, so he set off on his own. He never came back to the civilized world from his last adventure; however, his journal was found floating on the river one sunny day ten years, two months, and eleven days after he was declared missing.

* * *

His unforgettable journey, worthy of one of Jules Verne's novels, was inspirational to many anthropologists and explorers. It took Dr. J.'s colleagues nine years, two months, and eleven days to reach the conclusion that their honorable friend would indeed never come back. That was when he was declared missing or dead. Thirty-seven minutes after the publication of the memo from the society, a daring rescue attempt was organized and made by Dr. J.'s son, Dr. K. Burgess.

Dr. K., while holding the heaviest grudge against the scientists who would not accompany Dr. K., strongly believed that his genius father was still alive and was residing peacefully somewhere deep inside the Amazonian jungles. He knew that his father's knowledge was essential to humankind and significant to the betterment and progress of society, so he gathered some of the best anthropologists and explorers. The scientists, ashamed of having let Dr. J. go on the exploration on his own, accepted Dr. K.'s invitation and joined him on a quest to find the great doctor. To be clear, however, even this collaboration from the scientific community did not lessen Dr. K.'s grudge against them.

The extensive search took more than ten futile years; not only was there no sign of Dr. J., but Dr. K and his team of scientists were unable to make any scientific discovery worth studying.

Finally, the explorers decided it was time to give up. As they were about to start packing up, Dr. J.'s journal turned up floating on the river. Many years later one of the anthropologists remembered the glorious day on which Dr. K. spotted the journal drifting on the angry white waters of the Amazon. It was a sunny day, and the members of the expedition were ready to go back to where they had come from, when Dr. K. noticed the clean, dry, and inspirational journal floating on the water. It was almost an inch above the water.

Armed with the newfound motivation, Dr. K. made his most influential speech ever. He inspired the rest of the expedition team and helped them see the value of staying on course and continuing to search for the missing scientist. What Dr. K. found puzzling and yet did not feel compelled to share with anyone else was that several pages from the journal were missing.

The search took another twelve years, until Dr. K. was bitten by an infected female mosquito. At first it was like always, as though nothing had happened. He had killed the mosquito and wasn't even bothered by the idea that he was bitten. Then he started to sweat, which continued for four days in a row. At the end of the fourth day, he started a temperature; the fever stayed with him for two consecutive days, and then he was healthy again. No one noticed that he looked a little transparent after the episode finished. Two days later, he had another four-day period of sweating, which was immediately followed by a period of fever for exactly two days, and then he was healthy again for ten days before another episode started.

He yo-yoed from one condition to the other exactly twenty-one times, every time becoming more and more transparent, yet no one dared mention this to him. Before long he was so transparent that anyone could see through and inside him. Now that anybody could see right through him, it was obvious that he wasn't as good a person as he had once been thought to be. The grudge that he had been holding inside for so many years was quite visible. One of his friends later mentioned to a scientist that he'd known about the grudge, but he did not realize how big it had grown over the years. Soon, as Dr. K. became more transparent, the grudge started to lessen.

Finally, one Wednesday morning, he vanished as though he had never existed. The native helpers who were working at the camp reported that they saw the journal of Dr. J. take off and fly toward the sky slowly as Dr. K. started to vanish. The more transparent Dr. K. became, the closer the journal got to the sky. The day that Dr. K. disappeared was the day that the journal joined the blue sky and never came back.

The natives, having been part of the expedition for years, had learned what the journal really had to offer, and even now, fifty years later, they are sure that the journal will one day come back to reveal the secrets of a new world. The journal will guide them to a great land, a place that is not very far, not very near. It is not very hot and not very cold, a disease-free place where no one has to work and everyone, despite how he or she might look, is treated equally.

The family of Dr. J. and Dr. K. Burgess, on the other hand, enjoy their own perspective on this matter. Not long after the disappearance of Dr. K., his sister, pursuing the family tradition, acquired her degree in anthropology and followed in her brother's footsteps to find out what had happened to her father and brother. She, later known as Dr. L. Burgess, never left her hometown, yet only by studying her brother's notes and papers, she made an incredible discovery. Unfortunately for all of us, Dr. L. remained unaware that several pages of the journal were missing. Had she known, she would have probably uncovered the missing content through her research from her office as well.

* * *

Dr. L., since the time she was only a pudgy six-year-old, knew there was something fascinating about her family, and finally she had the chance to prove it and show it to the world. It took many sleepless nights as she went on devouring documents left from Dr. K. She attempted to find the hidden meanings of every note, every sentence; you might call her quest a series of unbelievable interpretations.

Regardless of what you might think, she continued on this path until her kind soul eventually finished the project. What she discovered and presented was highly regarded by her family and the close friends of the Burgess family.

In seeking a cure for the only fatal disease of his century, boredom, Dr. J. Burgess had set off on a journey — a journey that he knew would be a never-ending one, as he was never truly sure that undertaking such an arduous journey would be rewarded in any way. Throughout the journey he was repeatedly proven right that being resourceful was necessary but not enough. Believing in himself, he kept on going until one day, quite unexpectedly, he was handsomely rewarded.

He made the greatest discovery of the century. Yet he knew he could not share his finding with normal, ordinary people. The people were not mature enough to understand the meaning of his discovery. He therefore settled down in a remote place inside the Amazon, waiting for the right time when he could finally come out of hiding to share his discovery with the rest of humankind.

Dr. K., cherishing the hope that one day he would find his father, followed in his father's footsteps and made the same discovery. He too was very well aware of the undeveloped nature of humans; thus, he gracefully stepped out and joined his father in his reclusive hiding place. In this way he did not have to make any attempts to explain the unexplainable to the normal and ordinary people of his century. There they are waiting for the right moment when humanity has matured enough to understand what they discovered in the depth of the Amazonian jungles. When the right time arrives, they will deliver their friends and relatives to the best that world has to offer. Enjoying the ultimate knowledge, Drs. J. and K. Burgess are the only people who can recognize when the right time is.

Knowing how difficult it was for anyone to understand the contents of the journal of Dr. J., Dr. K. did not share the meaning of its content with fellow explorers. He knew that he did not have the right to share the secrets as they had been described in the journal with other scientists, for they were humans and hence undeveloped and unready. He would make hints to his fellow scientists. He would never communicate anything directly to anyone; however, he would write cryptic notes. These extensive notes remained long after his disappearance and were delivered to his sister.

Dr. J.'s journal described how to reach an island that is situated well beyond the discouraging forest of the dead. This is an island well hidden from our inquisitive eyes, a place that cannot be reached unless one has its accurate and precise direction, although even knowing the direction to this place is not entirely enough. To get to this place, not only should a seeker walk past the forest of the dead, but he or she will have to cross an acidic quagmire. If the mire doesn't devour the seeker, the compound will dissolve his or her body, and if the acid doesn't do enough damage, there are reptiles living beyond the quagmire to greet the explorer. These reptiles, whose shapes are mysterious to us, live only in this area.

If a traveler, by any divine help, travels past the reptile habitat, takes a right turn, and keeps walking until he or she gets to the knife stone and then takes another right turn and continues strolling, the individual will get to a swamp. This, however, is not an ordinary swamp. It covers a huge area. The thickness of the swamp makes it practically impossible for any living being to enter and successfully move in it. The swamp easily devours that which enters it.

Although the swamp is vast, it doesn't hide the island it surrounds behind the curvature of the earth. This island is oval shaped and can be very well seen from beyond the swamp; what a spectator notices about the island is how symmetrically it is surrounded and protected by the oldest trees that have ever existed and have survived the turbulent history of our blue planet. The trees are mangled and protect the island so that not even a worthless mosquito can get inside or out. What a spectator cannot see is that the dome of trees surrounds the island in a three-dimensional fashion. From above, the island looks like a giant green puff.

The island is utterly secluded from the outside; no one can ever enter or exit this natural prison. The thickness of the trees is so formidable that only a nuclear explosion might bring down that powerful barrier, and this is only a possibility.

Dr. Burgess senior was aware of what he had discovered. He knew he could never set foot on the island, and he knew he needed to wait for the right time to learn more about it, so he settled down where he could be close to this oval-shaped island. On this island lies a great secret that remained unknown to Dr. Burgess senior: the green, oval-shaped, natural Alcatraz is inhabited.

It is not known how anybody managed to get past all the barriers and chose to settle down on the island. A theory is that the so-called natural barriers were constructed by the first inhabitants of the island. They came to the island and constructed the barriers to protect themselves; over the years, they intentionally or unintentionally forgot about life outside their green island.

Another theory states that some other beings, knowledgeable and fearless creatures with power and determination beyond our imagination, brought the first people to the island and constructed all sorts of barriers to protect them from the dangers of the world, as we would do for our beloved pets.

Life on the island might have emerged easily with only a handful of Homo sapiens running away from a dreadful animal, fearing for their lives. The natural protective fence could have come into existence long after, trapping them and their descendants gradually on the island. Our ancestors were quite uneducated in the field of freedom and all its related topics, and they may not have cared that the island was constructing an impenetrable wall around them until it was too late.

Despite the manner in which the first people arrived and how or why they stayed isolated and secluded from the rest of the world, life did not take a different path on the island. There are many similarities between life on and off the island. As Samuel Butler once wrote, "All progress is based upon a universal innate desire on the part of every organism to live beyond its income."[2] People on the green island made staggering progress, as staggering a progress as the people outside the green island made. We all took different paths but arrived at the same destination at relatively the same time.

Today we are unaware of this island. We have grown, and we have made countless achievements. They too have grown and made countless achievements. We are, one way or another, proud of our empty accomplishments, and yet there is an undiscovered piece of land on our planet where its inhabitants have no evidence that they share the universe with others. Ironically, we have no evidence that we share our universe with them either.

---

[2] Samuel Butler, *The Note-books of Samuel Butler* (New York: E.P. Dutton & Co., 1917), 12.

2 — *The City of Hay'at*

People on the oval-shaped island had lived in one city for thousands of years before the city was broken in two, but that is a story for another time. Suffice it to say for now that every organism will have to eventually be broken in two if it wants to evolve and more importantly if it wants to survive, and a flourishing city is no exception.

Having resided on the island for thousands of years, the island dwellers have no concept of words such as *city, town, sea, ocean,* or even *island*. Being unique does not eliminate the need for a name, however. Naming shows the respect people have for their beloved objects. The inhabitants of the island are no exceptions; they have developed the ultimate respect for the place in which they live, and over the years they coined a word in their language for this place: *Hay'at*. *Hay'at* could be the closest word in Sokaji, the language of the island dwellers, to *center*.

The city of Hay'at is located in the middle of the island; to its people is situated in the center of the universe. No matter where anybody starts sightseeing or what road they take on the island, that road will eventually reach the city of Hay'at. And that is what the name conveys: a place that exists in the middle of the universe, regardless of how small or large this universe is.

Hay'at is not a vast city; with the current population of 208,104, it is a medium to small city. There is no similarity between the city and its people. The Hay'aties are very warm and hospitable on the inside as well as the outside.

The city, although gorgeous on the inside, does not possess an attractive façade, for it is located on the formidable oval-shaped island, surrounded by an impenetrable wall of trees. To the Hay'aties, who cannot see their beloved city from the outside, their homeland truly deserves the adjective *gorgeous*. It is a shame that no one from outside has ever managed to visit the city; they would have been accepted with warm welcomes.

The city of Hay'at moves neither in time nor space; it, therefore, exists in a timeless time and a spaceless space, engraving its history in the course of the universe in a language no one registers or understands. Yet the time and space in which the city exists are of no importance. That the city exists is all that matters.

The Hay'aties have achieved an inconceivable amount of social and scientific progress. Could it be possible for people stranded on a desert island to make such progress? Shouldn't they be condemned and doomed to live like bedouins until the end of time? One could argue that humankind was left alone on earth, and they managed to make headway in more ways than one; one could also argue that with all our headway, we are still bedouins in jeans and t-shirts. We tend to characterize a civilization by the amount of progress it has made, yet progress remains a relative concept. The distinctive feature of our civilization is progress in its form rather than making progress. All beings, in every shape and form, spend their lives in efforts to narrow the gap between convenience and inconvenience, and they call the result progress.

To the Hay'aties, convenience is to fly beyond their island and explore what exits outside it. Inconvenience, on the other hand, is the fact that the protective trees around the island are impenetrable. There are folk stories about how, once upon a time, there was a small opening to the world outside of the island, and that opening has long since been closed by the massive branches of the island's protective trees. This opening, it is said, was in the middle of the island. The yellow rays of the gods outside the island would come down to the surface of the island through this opening. No one knows when or how this opening was closed; neither does anyone know if this could ever be reopened one day. There are folk stories about how this opening might one day return and bring the majestic yellow rays with it.

For hundreds of years, since they managed to fly for the first time, the Hay'aties have tried to break free and leave the island to go beyond the trees and explore the outside world. For some it has become their lives' obsession to learn more about the universe—the world outside. They have developed elaborate theories on various other universes that exist in parallel to their own island universe. To prove or disprove any of these theories, they, of course, need to travel beyond their island and visit the outside world. So they set out to find a way to leave the island; they made thousands of discoveries and inventions in the process, none of which helped them to leave.

Soon leaving the island proved impossible; the trees proved to be so protective of the Hay'aties that they had to give up and accept the reality that there was no outside to their world and that they were the only creatures in the universe. From one perspective, this disproved all the theories that they had regarding other universes. Logically, if they couldn't leave the island, that would mean that there was nothing outside of the island, and if there was nothing outside of the island, then that meant there were no other universes in existence. This sad realization did not lessen the importance of all other discoveries that they had made along the way. When their first flying machine flew above the heads of the inhabitants, people were so excited that they would point to their green sky and would only be able to utter the excited sound of "ooh." Soon, it was people just pointing to flying machines and uttering the sound of "ooh." The young Hay'aties, not having any other word, would just emphasize the sound of "ooh" and point to the flying machine whenever they saw one. It is no wonder that today the Sokaji word for a flying machine is *ooh'eh*.

A few decades after the realization that there were no other universes in existence, Samari'eh, one of the most accomplished writers and philosophers of the city of Hay'at, wrote, "For life in the city of Hay'at, gods themselves fight." The day Samari'eh shared his thoughts was the day that the Hay'aties really and truly understood the significance of life on the island and that the island was genuinely a heaven. Some pessimists marked that day as the day it was categorically proven that they were imprisoned on the island. The optimists and true believers, on the other hand, knew they were the only creatures in the universe. Since then they have been seriously busy trying to understand the meaning of life. They took this upon themselves to make life easier for generations to come.

The Hay'aties enjoy a rich and deep culture. This new angle toward looking at life descends from the simple fact that they cannot conceive of many concepts we find ordinary. The notions of blue sky along with snow, rain, the sun, the moon, or stars, although tangible for us, remain abstract concepts to them. There is only the minute reflection of the sun penetrating through the thousand-year-old mammoth trees that makes their atmosphere look green and symbolizes the start of their day.

Although snow and rain are as mysterious to them as oxygen to...well, whatever organism does not require oxygen, the illegitimate son of water and soil is not a mystery to them. Water conspires with soil to make mud, the birthplace of bacteria, and the damp weather would make people susceptible to the worst diseases. The close relationship that they developed with tropical diseases became the greatest encouragement for them to spend many years working in the field of medicine to discover the cures to their once-terminal diseases. Eventually menaces that had plagued them for generations became only nuances that every now and then they would experience. Now they are more concerned with longevity, which has driven them to make incredible breakthroughs. They have evolved since the dark ages, when they did not know how to cure the common cold. As a result of many discoveries in this field, they have managed to increase their life expectancy. Nowadays living to the ripe age of 120 of their years is quite ordinary.

Being inside the enormous set of trees and in the middle of a tropical river, the city of Hay'at experiences only two seasons: the hot season and the mild season, each of which lasts only four of our months. They developed the concept of a year, which consists of eight of their months.

The Hay'aties have slanted the philosophy of life in their own favor. They accept the fact that they are the only intelligent beings living in a small universe and that the universe is not large enough to accommodate other intelligent species. However, some of their intellectual thinkers, as one would expect, muse that people should keep open minds as to other possibilities and to the fact that someday the bases of their beliefs might change, and some radical thinkers and philosophers every now and then come up with more drastic ideas. In spite of all the facts that exist, they even boldly reject the most fundamental ideas such as being alone in the universe, the fact that the universe was created only for them, and that they are the only chosen creatures of the gods; they strongly believe these ideas to be nothing short of preposterous. Over the years, the people of Hay'at have started to call the most successful of such philosophers the "chosen ones."

Not only have the people of Hay'at made amazing progress in physical sciences and art, but they have made advancements in their social science as well; for instance, they developed a structured government, consisting of two different levels. Every one thousand people in the city of Hay'at have a representative in the House of Representatives. Each fifty representatives have one representative in the House of Elders. The House of Representatives is responsible for governing the city. The main responsibility of the House of Elders is to consider the best candidates and then select one of them as the chosen one during the New Year celebration.

The tradition of selecting the chosen one is rather a modern occurrence in the history of the island, while the New Year celebration is something that has been perfected over thousands of years of living there. The celebration, which takes exactly fourteen days, starts seven days before the end of the mild season and continues into the hot season.

The significances of the festival are countless. Adults love the festival as well as children do. Some love it because they can relax; some like it because they can drink and dance for days on end. Some love this time of the year because it is when the candidates for the chosen one are selected; to them the excitement and the thrill of this ritual is the greatest entertainment. Even though the selection of candidates is not publicly announced, people generally learn who they are, and this is when the suspense and speculations fill the air of the city. People even make bets on which of the candidates will be the one actually chosen for the year. This becomes the cornerstone of the New Year celebrations. The final selection is the result of full deliberations of the members of the House of Elders. They consider many aspects and criteria during their deliberations to make a final selection on who the chosen one for the year will be. While the details of the selection process remain unknown to the ordinary Hay'aties, the citizens of the city know that the most important thing for the members of the House of Elders is to be fair in their final selection.

The announcement of the names of the candidates is not glamorous at all. As a matter of fact, only the candidates are made aware of their candidacy. Many candidates choose to share this honor and joyful news with their family and friends while they anxiously await the final result. In the city of Hay'aties, the idea of whether or not sharing anticipation with others will cause the outcome to fall through is a personal belief. Hence, while many gladly and proudly share this news, many would rather not do so in hopes that this will increase their chances of success.

Being the chosen one has many benefits. For one, the chosen ones get to be buried in the only cemetery that the city of Hay'at has: Kabaro'ostan. Having inadequate space, the Hay'aties prefer to cremate their dead unless the dead is a chosen one. Once a person is chosen, he or she becomes a part of the history of the city of Hay'at. All the chosen ones are equal, so no names or other personal information is engraved on their tombstones. A number is the only piece of information that the tombstone will hold; consequently, when visitors step through the majestic gates of Kabaro'ostan and enter the cemetery, they see series of small, numbered stones, each representing a chosen one. For many Hay'aties, especially the elderly, spending a day at Kabaro'ostan with their friends and deliberating on the past and the future is deeply meaningful. They sometimes get together, go on a picnic, find a nice place at the cemetery, have something to eat, and discuss anything that comes to mind.

Unlike the announcement of the candidates, which remains rather personal, announcing the chosen one is one of the most appealing events devised by any society. Once the name of the lucky individual is announced, it is all glamour, fame, and fortune for the person.

For someone to be selected as a candidate, he or she needs to be between twenty-seven and fifty-four years of age (by his or her own measurement) and has to have raised serious questions against the philosophy of life in the city of Hay'at. The more serious and the more belief-shattering a person's questions are, the more it is possible that he or she will become the chosen one.

Half a day before the beginning of the New Year, the members of the House of Elders announce the name of the selected individual. This is a most thrilling and heart-melting event. For years to come, fathers will make bedtime stories of the event to tell their children and the children of their children.

The event begins when the head of the House of Elders, known as the chief, sets foot on the Platform of Time to announce the name of the fortunate individual. No one knows when the Platform of Time was built, but everybody knows what purpose it serves. This is where the chief rewards the chosen one. Once the chief sets foot on the first of the 104 steps leading to the 108-foot-high platform, everybody becomes quiet. By the time the chief reaches the platform, the air is saturated with curiosity.

The audience, gasping, waits until the chief opens his mouth and says the words they find endearing, the words for which they have been waiting. Once the chief announces the name of the chosen one, there is cheering mixed with jealousy, joy, and relief. The smell of jealousy and respect fills the air. Those who have yearned to be chosen feel the jealousy, and those who are close to the chosen one feel the joy. Some people, on the other hand, feel relief.

As the announcement is made, words leave the chief's mouth; they travel at the speed of sound and throw away everyone and everything on their way. These words are on a mission to find the owner of the name. Once the words find the person they have been looking for, they grasp him or her firmly by the neck and drag him or her to the steps of the Platform of Time. As the happy chosen one climbs up the steps, escorted by the sacred words of the chief, he or she savors the joy, and enjoys the jealousy.

Once on the platform, the chosen one can see how much the Hay'aties love him or her and how important he or she is to the progress of their society.

A group of specially trained young people escort the chosen one to the special place, where the chosen one will be treated like the special person he or she really is. The person will be served the most scrumptious food and wine: pheasant, liverwurst, island caviar, and truffles. While in the spa, the chosen one will have friends and close relatives come to visit so they can enjoy having a chosen one in their family; the nearest and dearest try to find out the true secret of becoming the chosen one. They too want to become chosen ones before it is too late. The chosen one is ordinarily kind enough to communicate well to the unfortunate ones how he or she managed to arrive at this heavenly status.

The treatment and heavenly living eventually end, as all good things do, and the chosen one walks back to the Platform of Time when it is close to the New Year. Music is loud, and there are breathtaking fireworks; people are either passed out from drinking or on their way to the land of the unconscious.

The ritual includes a stool and the sacred rope. The chosen one sets a foot on the stool. The chief puts the noose of the sacred rope around the neck of the chosen one. The chief addresses the audience, conveying to the Hay'aties how important they and their society are and how lucky the society is to have developed such a chosen one, someone who takes his or her responsibilities seriously and undertakes them with utmost dedication. The chief pushing the chosen one off the stool does not mark the end of the celebration. In fact, that is probably the least important aspect of the ceremony. The audience members keep on enjoying themselves for hours after.

Since the ritual of finding and selecting a chosen one in the city of Hay'at started, there have never been any relatives or close friends of the members of the House of Elders among the candidates. The members are very careful not to give rise to the notion that they play favoritism in any way; those who have the power to select the chosen one are just, and they rightly believe that selecting someone in their close circles, even as a candidate, could shatter the sanctity of the process. They rightly believe that the fairness of the process needs to be maintained. Yet this is not a law on the island, so when, some time ago, the son of one of the members of the House of Elders was selected as a candidate to become the chosen one, those who found out were shocked, but they accepted the fact regardless. People did not expect that he would be the chosen one anyway. His selection as the chosen one would certainly have been unfair—not illegal, just unfair.

When Nasha'at, son of honorable Msa'adam, was announced as one of the candidates, to prove the sanctity of the ritual and to show that no one influences the result of the selection, his father took it upon himself to take a few days off, stay away from the House of Elders, and let his fellow elders make their decision without him. The other members started their deliberations to determine who would be the chosen one for the year without Msa'adam.

At the time that the deliberation was happening, Nasha'at, his father, and his mother were on the far side of the island in their cottage. Nasha'at, deep down, yearned to become the chosen one; his father, on the other hand, was sure that his son would not become that; he had made some arrangements to make sure this would not happen.

"The sanctity of our society will be in danger," he had told the other members of the House of Elders. "We cannot take away this opportunity from the rest of the citizens; we cannot and should not do something that would look like favoritism in the eyes of history."

Nasha'at's mother had learned over the years that whatever her husband tried to achieve was for the betterment of his family and his society, so she would agree with her husband, although she could not conceal the fact that she wanted her son to be happy, and her son clearly desired to become the chosen one. At the same time, she was one of those Hay'aties who would feel relief in the mixture of emotions if someone they knew was not selected as the chosen one.

3 — Nasha'at and Msa'adam

Nasha'at had just turned thirty. The feeling of reaching the age of thirty, in any measurement, is a defining feeling. One who is in one's twenties lives on a separate planet from the rest of the population and, like an extraterrestrial critic, takes a seat up in heaven and looks down at the pitiful lives of the rest of the human race, wondering why everyone fails to see what he or she can see. Such a person finds the sky to be the limit and decides that rules are to be broken and accepted conventions to be redefined. At thirty the page turns; one comes down from one's throne and becomes more and more worried about terrestrial matters. Principles don't preoccupy as much as they used to; at this age of reckoning, one thinks more about earthly matters than heavenly subjects; one is reborn.

Nasha'at was at this time of life. He had had his opportunity to look at his society from his throne. Since he turned thirty, he realized how important it was to have a family of his own and to take care of his own clan, his job, and his duties. There was a time when he would spend his life trying to change the way his people saw, felt about, and conceived of their world; this now was ancient history.

A few weeks before, Nasha'at had learned that he was one of the lucky and fortunate candidates for the year. The news had an incredible effect on him. Although he was not involved in anything worth candidacy as of late, he felt he had contributed enough to his society in the past to be selected as a candidate. For years, he had questioned every foundational part of the Hay'aties' society; there was not even a nail in the pillars of Hay'ati wisdom that he had left untouched. He had even questioned his father's place in the House of Elders. Considering what he had done over the years, deep down in his heart of hearts, he felt not only did he deserve the candidacy but that he was worthy of being selected as the chosen one.

"We'd better go back to the celebration," Nasha'at said to his father.

"Why? You are tired of the cottage?" Msa'adam said sarcastically.

"I remember when you only wanted to spend your time here," Nasha'at's mother said, giving him a meaningful look.

"It is not like that," Nasha'at said.

"You are hoping you will be the chosen one, aren't you?" Msa'adam's voice was hysterical. "I told you it is not going to happen."

"Why? Why do you think I don't deserve to be the chosen one?"

"It is not that you don't deserve that. You should not...you *must* not become the chosen one. You are my son." Msa'adam breathed. "You are not even supposed to become a candidate."

"It doesn't matter what I or you feel and want. If I am to be the chosen one, I *will* be selected. Now all I am thinking about is the celebration," he lied. "At least we can go back to the celebration and enjoy ourselves."

That was how they decided to leave their cottage on the far side of the island to go back and join the celebration. Msa'adam knew that his son would not be selected as the chosen one; he kept telling himself that he had done everything in his power to make sure this would not happen.

Then again, we should go back. I need to see the chief and make sure they have not selected Nasha'at as their so-called chosen one, and if they have, maybe I can change their decision. No announcement has been made yet; there is still time. We need to go back right now, he told himself. *The sanctity of our society will be in danger.*

The more he thought about that, the more he felt uneasy. *What if they have chosen Nasha'at? No, they couldn't have. What if they have made a decision that will shatter the trust of people? What if...what if...?*

As soon as they were back, Msa'adam rushed to see the other members of the House of Elders, his heart in his mouth. On his way to the house, he looked at people, some yanking vegetables from the ground and making jokes, some drinking and dancing, some walking and talking quietly, and some shouting rambunctiously. He had butterflies in his stomach. He held his hand on his stomach to calm the butterflies down. It was no use; they absorbed the warmth of his hands and started to fly more vigorously.

As Msa'adam was about to enter the House of Elders, three old ladies standing by the door of the house caught his attention.

"H-h-he...is g-g-g-going to be s-s-s-surp-p-pr-rised," the first woman stammered very quietly.

Msa'adam either didn't hear her or decided to ignore her.

"I tell you — I tell you there is nothing he can do. I tell you," said the second one. She was speaking with the speed of light. Ordinary people's ears would not register what she had to say.

The third lady just shook her head.

He entered the house and walked straight to the meeting room, where he knew the rest of the members would be. He opened the door and looked at the elders, one of whom was wearing the chief's hat.

"Congratulations, my old friend," the chief said cheerfully. "It is decided: your son is going to be the chosen one. It is a great honor."

Msa'adam was flabbergasted. For a few seconds, he forgot to breathe. As his face was turning blue, he remembered that the distance between life and death is only one breath, so he started to breathe again. He needed to be alive to explain to the rest of the elders the error of their ways.

"It was not an easy decision, but we have collectively agreed that Nasha'at is the perfect choice," continued the chief.

"But you had promised not to choose my son," said Msa'adam, panting. "Never has any relative of the elders been selected as the chosen one. This is not right; this is not fair. It is not too late yet; you should—you *have to* change your vote."

"That's not happening," said the elder on the chief's right side. "We had this discussion over and over; he is the chosen one."

"But he is my son," Msa'adam breathed.

"And that is not going to change anything," said the other elder, his sharp words ripping Msa'adam's heart apart. "We are going to announce the result tomorrow."

Msa'adam felt that his heart was heavy and bleeding. He moved his hand over his chest. He felt his heartbeat going fast. Then he moved his hand close to the front of his face to look at it. His hand was warm, wet, and red; it was his own blood on his hand. "That is not fair," he repeated. "Please, you have to understand; that is not fair."

The chief shrugged.

Msa'adam realized there was nothing he could do. With his head down, he repeated, "The sanctity of our society will be in danger."

He felt that he heard someone asking, "Is that what you really care about right now?"

He had to rush back home and talk to his son. He could hide him; there was still a lot they could do. He turned and walked toward the door.

"You understand that you need to keep this a secret until tomorrow," said the chief. "People work the whole year waiting for this day, and we don't want to spoil their fun."

"Yes," continued another elder. "Even your son should not know about his selection until tomorrow."

Msa'adam looked at them, emotionless.

"You are not going to do something foolish to disgrace yourself, your son, and the rest of your family forever, are you?" the chief said as Msa'adam was leaving the room.

Msa'adam didn't reply.

Years later, when he met the wolf, Msa'adam remembered that day; he could remember the details of that day and what exactly happened, but he couldn't remember how he got to his home from the House of Elders.

At home Nasha'at was reading a book, and his mother was cooking. "You...we have to leave right now," Msa'adam said impatiently. "Gather your things; we have to go somewhere. I don't know where yet." He was still in shock.

"What is going on?" asked Nasha'at. "I have never seen you like this."

"You have been selected to be the chosen one."

"That's incredible." Nasha'at chuckled. "I had my hopes, but I didn't think, not even for a second, that I might be lucky enough to be selected as the chosen one."

"We have to leave now," Msa'adam said categorically.

His wife looked at him emotionlessly.

"Are you jealous?" Nasha'at asked indifferently. "That's it, isn't it? You are jealous of me and that I'm being selected as the chosen one, and you have never even gotten close to this position."

"Don't be ridiculous. Come on; let's go."

"I don't know what to say." Nasha'at was furious. "You are my father; you should be proud of me and what I have become. Yet you envy what I have achieved." Nasha'at paused for a second. "I am not going anywhere, and I can't look at you right now. I don't want to see you. I'm not sure if I want to have a father who is jealous of his son." Nasha'at was disgusted, and he was gone.

Msa'adam's heart was bleeding again. He sat down, propping his head on his hands. "That's not fair," he said. "That is *not* fair. The sanctity of our society will be in danger." He had hoped he could take his son out of the ritual, but his hope now was only a dream. He could see that the process had started, and there was nothing he could do to stop it.

As Nasha'at was leaving his father's house, three old ladies standing near the house saw him.

"He…is…t-t-tired," stammered the first lady.

"I tell you—I tell you he is disgusted. I tell you," said the second lady with the speed of light.

The third lady looked at him and shook her head.

* * *

Msa'adam did not see his son until the next day, right after the chief had announced his name.

The day of the announcement was as chaotic as always. Children were playing everywhere, creating a sort of pandemonium that parents love when their own kids create and hate when other children do. Msa'adam could remember the days when Nasha'at was one of those kids, running around, not caring about the superficial problems of life, and only trying to have fun. Those days were ancient history to him now. *I'm going to cut those days out of my memory, frame them, and hang them on the wall,* he thought. *I want to keep those magical days alive forever.*

Msa'adam had not been sleeping since he'd heard that Nasha'at was going to be selected as the chosen one. He had tried to see his son but with no luck; he wanted to persuade his son to run away, to disgrace himself and his family and not to become the chosen one. Nasha'at, knowing what Msa'adam had planned, had not agreed to see his father. Nasha'at knew the honorable Msa'adam was jealous of him. The generation gap between them was now as spacious as a canyon.

Msa'adam knew the only way he could get to his son and meet him would be after the announcement. Despite the hatred his son might have for him, he would accept his father like anyone else and would listen to him. He waited until the chief had announced Nasha'at as the chosen one, and then he followed his son to the spa they had prepared for him.

As Msa'adam was walking toward the spa, he noticed the three old ladies by its door. "It is...g-g-g-going to b-b-be ug-g-gly," stammered the first one.

"I tell you—I tell you he is going to abuse his powers. I tell you," said the second lady.

The third lady only shook her head.

Msa'adam entered the building with a warm, yellowish, formidable air. Everybody knew the honorable Msa'adam, a member of the House of Elders. They all had the utmost respect for him, and looking at him, they realized he wanted to be alone with his son. Msa'adam hadn't realized yet that Nasha'at was no longer just his son. He was the chosen one now, and he belonged to all the Hay'aties.

Once everybody had left, Nasha'at looked at Msa'adam and gracefully said, "Hello, Father." His grace was bluish and cold. It was incredibly influential and formidable—even more formidable than the air Msa'adam was emitting. It took a fraction of a moment for Msa'adam's yellow aura to be entirely consumed by his son's blue aura. The room's light became noticeably cold and blue.

"Son, you have to leave with me right now," begged Msa'adam; without the formidable air, Msa'adam was an ordinary person. "You have to understand, my son, my dear son; please leave with me before it is too late."

Nasha'at looked at his father. "Do you really understand what it is that you are asking me to do?" Nasha'at asked calmly. "You want me to step back from my responsibilities and disappoint my people. How could you live with a disgraced son like that? Are you jealous of me. You should be proud that I, your son, have been selected as the chosen one. Outside this place, the world is waiting for me." Nasha'at was pointing at the window. "My people believe in me; they are sure I have earned it to be rightfully named the chosen one. Why aren't you?"

"That is not fair," cried Msa'adam. "That is not fair. You are my only son."

"I think you should leave now, Father." Nasha'at was still calm. "We don't have much to discuss, and I have to get ready."

Msa'adam dragged himself out of the building; he could hardly walk, but he managed to get to the base of the Platform of Time. His wife was standing and waiting for him. Msa'adam looked at his wife. She had the face of an angel, calm and hopeful, yet this time there was nothing to hope for.

"That is not fair," said Msa'adam as his wife hugged him. "That is not fair."

* * *

A few hours later, Msa'adam and his wife could see their son coming onto the Platform of Time. He looked powerful, thoughtful, and very handsome; he was like a blossoming bud. He moved his arms toward people kindly and smiled at children. He was demonstrating his attitude, his leadership. The cheers were deafening. When Nasha'at reached the platform, there were the most amazing fireworks. The Hay'aties were clearly happy about the choice the elders had made. They had known Nasha'at since he was young, and they had loved him. For many years, they had listened to what he had to say, had thought about the meaning of what he had to tell them, and now they very well believed he deserved to be the chosen one. Now that the selection had happened, no one thought that selecting the son of an elder would damage the foundations of their society.

He set foot on the steps of the platform, and people cheered even more. He waved to people. As he climbed up the stairs, he felt that his existence was merging with the existence of the other chosen ones. They were part of a collective, all immortal; he was stepping onto a higher level of existence.

High on the platform, the chief was waiting for him and greeted him with open arms and an attractive smile. The chief guided Nasha'at to the stool and helped him stand on it. Nasha'at proudly stretched his arms out and smiled at his people.

The people of Hay'at were cheering and drinking; there was loud music, to which some people were dancing.

Some kids were playing not very far from the platform. They were all joyful and pleased. There was incredible energy being emitted from the crowd. Nasha'at, while having his arms stretched out, took a deep breath, trying to inhale as much energy as he could. "The people of Hay'at...*my* people, I now belong to you!" Nasha'at shouted to the crowd.

Somewhere in the crowd, Msa'adam was standing next to his wife, looking at Nasha'at. "That is not fair," he said for the last time. His wife looked at him and suddenly burst into tears. There were three old ladies standing next to them.

"She is t-t-t-t-tired of her husb-b-band," stuttered the first lady.

"I tell you—I tell you she is jealous; I tell you," gasped the second one.

"She is just sad," mused the third lady.

The ritual was reaching its climax. Up on the platform, Nasha'at was looking proudly at his people. The sacred rope was around his neck, and he was wearing a timeless smile. Down in the crowd, people had either passed out or were unconsciously dancing to different rhythms and tunes. The fireworks were becoming more and more beautiful and eye catching; the display was exciting and spectacular. Small kids were staring at the fireworks, gasping and screaming in pleasure.

Finally, the time everybody had been waiting for arrived: the finale of the fireworks.

Traditionally, there are 208 consecutive, elaborate projectiles exploding in the air to produce 208 different displays, the most amazing sight that anybody hopes to see. The most important one of those projectiles is number 104. That is the number that everyone on the island anxiously expects to see.

The final fireworks started, the first, second, third. Joyful noises were coming from every corner, and then it was the 101st. It was getting closer to the number that everybody was excitedly waiting for. As it was getting closer, people were becoming quieter and quieter. Many had stopped breathing well before the 101st projectile. Even small children were quiet. The music had stopped. No one was saying anything; maybe they were waiting for someone to drop the pin. They wanted to hear the pin drop.

103...it was awfully close. 104—the magic number that the Hay'aties and their chosen one were waiting for had finally arrived. The chief, who was standing next to Nasha'at, pushed him off the stool with a swift move. The city of Hay'at exploded in cheers and joy. The fireworks continued their impressive and effective display until the 208th rocket was fired.

The next morning, Nasha'at was taken to Kabaro'ostan and was buried under number 624.

* * *

For the next 104 months, Msa'adam worked hard and lobbied until he successfully introduced a new law to the Hay'ati legal system. The city had grown and matured and was ready to replicate. Msa'adam's new law broke the city of Hay'at into two smaller flourishing and growing organisms: Upper Hay'at and Lower Hay'at. This was the most respectable accomplishment of the old Msa'adam. He had offered a choice to the citizens of his city. Those who would feel joy or jealousy at the ritual of the chosen one would stay in Upper Hay'at; those who would feel relief would move to live in Lower Hay'at. Those who wanted to be a chosen one would stay in the upper side. Those who felt that being the chosen one did not offer them anything of importance would move to the lower side. People of Hay'at now had a choice.

Msa'adam left the House of the Elders and focused his life on this new mission. He was selected as a candidate to be the chosen one three times, three years in a row. He never found out why he was not selected as the chosen one. Sometimes he felt he deserved more than anyone else to become the chosen one.

After 104 months, Msa'adam's efforts paid off. The House of the Elders allowed him and his followers to set up a new city south of the city of Hay'at, where there was less clean water, more mud, and more disease. They knew they had difficult lives ahead of them. No one blamed their loved ones who didn't join them. Msa'adam's wife was one of those nearest and dearest who decided to remain in Upper Hay'at.

The following year, when she was selected as the chosen one, she didn't know whether to feel joy, jealousy, or relief. She was very confused at the time.

Part 2

The Apple

4 — Zula'kier

Zula'kier wasn't your average Hay'ati. He had spent most of his twenty-six years traveling between the two cities on the oval-shaped island and studying. He was one of the most educated and knowledgeable people in both Upper and Lower Hay'at. He had studied Hay'ati social sciences and had graduated with the highest honors.

His father was a very well-respected negotiator. Zula'kier and his family had left Upper Hay'at when he was very young and set off to rediscover the oval-shaped island. In years to come, his father was stationed in Lower Hay'at. That had given Zula'kier the amazing opportunity to learn firsthand what Lower Hay'at had to offer. He had decided to stay in the lower side and continue his studies for a few more years after his parents had gone back to the upper side.

The brilliant educational background that Zula'kier had under his belt had helped him easily climb up the ladder of progress.

Young societies value education and credentials more; such societies are thirsty for progress, as Lower Hay'at was. The city was not as well off as the upper side was, with its rich history and powerful supporters. The lower side had started from the swamps of the upper side, and the lower side would welcome any addition to its knowledge base with open arms.

Despite all of his credentials and experiences, Zula'kier was rather a modest and down-to-earth professional. Although living in the lower side, he was as conservative as any Upper Hay'ati was.

A true Hay'ati conservative doesn't actually know that he or she is really conservative; on the contrary, such types feel that they are not conservative at all. These Hay'aties are more prevalent in the upper side; it is rare to see one in Lower Hay'at. Since the inception of Lower Hay'at, many changes had happened in this small society. The citizens had learned a great deal more about their own potential. They had discovered new areas in their own social sciences that, up to the birth of the lower side, they hadn't known even existed. As much the upper side was interested in its own ways, the lower side was interested in discovering new ways.

Real Upper Hay'aties hide behind a stone wall of modesty and pretend that it is politeness and not fright that encourages them to stick with the old way. You have to get very close to them, develop a deep sense of rapport and friendship, before they finally feel comfortable and slowly convey their true selves. Patience is the key. A student of Hay'ati social sciences can learn a great deal from a Hay'ati conservative.

Now that the contrast between the two sides had become noticeable, it made sense why a thoughtful, decent Hay'ati in the upper side would accept all the decisions made by the Houses of Representatives and Elders without refuting any of those decisions—because no self-respecting Hay'ati from the upper side wanted to run the risk of making an elder dislike him or her. Surmising that the average Upper Hay'ati has always been a slave to the more strong-willed members of the governing body of the city is not entirely inconceivable.

Do they follow others and their elders blindly? Yes. Don't they have any ideas of their own? The answer again is, of course, yes. They have brains, and they are capable of reflecting on life; that is why they produce enough candidates to be chosen ones. They just don't want to lose their cozy and comfortable lives.

Zula'kier accepted the Upper Hay'aties' way of life without question, regardless of whether he was living in the upper or lower side. He had a very well-defined set of values, and he was clear in his mind on what was right or wrong; the way of life in the upper side was right, and the more he lived in the lower side, the more he believed that. He didn't necessarily believe that the way of the lower siders was wrong. To him, it was a different way of life. It was just not the right way.

Zula'kier did know that the two societies had been founded on the same set of ideas. However, after thousands of years, the ideas had grown and multiplied; there was no longer room for all the ideas to live in one city. Hence, the city of Hay'at had multiplied. This way there would be enough room for all sorts of new ideas.

Our island dwellers have always considered the world as binary. There were always two distinct solutions to every challenge. The first solution would fit within the laws of the upper side, and the other one would be acceptable in the lower side.

In a place such as this secluded island, the only way to construct a thriving civilization was to bring people together on the basis of the ideas that they shared and offer them the opportunity to collaborate with one another in safeguarding those valuable ideas.

5 — Ki-Ham

Ki-Ham wasn't your average Hay'ati either. His main defining characteristic was that he didn't have any faith, neither in Upper nor Lower Hay'at—none whatsoever. He was definitely not as educated as Zula'kier was. He, however, would never accept or, even worse, confess that he didn't know the answer to any inquiry. Using his gift of gab, he could one way or another keep his addressees occupied. Ki-Ham was a living, breathing idea factory.

Since he subscribed to neither governing idea on the island, he could lead an easier lifestyle. Living on an island where the most precious commodities are ideas, one would not even consider leading a life independent from any of such ideas. To Ki-Ham, on the other hand, it was not so farfetched. It was just that. He felt right at home in Lower Hay'at, where people were more tolerant of unorthodox ideas.

It was an incredible time, one of great discoveries. Once upon a time, when there was only one city on the island, the citizens would collaborate and focus more to make headway in various fields of sciences. Now that the city had grown and replicated, there was an opportunity for all citizens to experiment with the two sides of the city of Hay'at—the old and the new—and step into a series of never-ending journeys of self-discovery. Ki-Ham wanted to explore every possible idea.

Ki-Ham believed in free will in its entirety. Hence, he decided to move out of his city and live temporarily in the upper side. He wanted to exercise his free will. He soon discovered that the air tasted different in the upper side. The air there would give him indigestion. Therefore, he rather quickly traveled back to his hometown. Yet while he was in the upper side, his philosophy of life started to change. This was the point in time when the foundation of his perspective on life changed. This new foundation was the platform for many new ideas that were born in his head in years to come. Right before his indigestion started and forced him to run back home, he shared one of his new ideas with the citizens of the upper side, an idea that was in direct conflict with everything that had encouraged him to live in the lower side and reside (at least temporarily) in the upper side in the first place. The idea shocked him more than anyone else.

He shared, "We, the island dwellers, are too vain to accept that there is no freedom of will." Poor Ki-Ham—he hadn't the slightest idea that someone else in a different and parallel universe and at an unknown time wrote, "The strongest knowledge (that of the total unfreedom of the human will) is nonetheless the poorest in successes, for it always has the strongest opponent, human vanity."[3] This confusion, nevertheless, remained with him to the last moment of his life. He could not decide whether there was or was not free will for the citizens of the island. This, however, is a story for another time.

Ki-Ham wanted to learn everything. He certainly had an opinion on everything. Ordinarily, when an individual tries to learn as many topics as possible, he or she ends up only scratching the surface of the topics. To fill in the gaps in his or her knowledge, then, he or she ends up

---

[3]Friedrich Nietzsche, *Human, All-Too-Human, A Book For Free Spirits Part II*, trans. Paul V. Cohn, B.A. (New York: The MacMillan Company, 1913), 36.

making many incorrect assumptions. Many will eventually give up and be content with the broken pieces they have already learned; therefore, their deductions will be based on incomplete knowledge levels. Since having insufficient knowledge is more dangerous than a total lack of knowledge, the deductions of such jacks-of-all-trades are not to be entirely trusted, no matter how convincing such individuals might sound while trying to express their perspectives and prove that their judgments are indeed correct. And Ki-Ham could be very convincing.

Unlike Zula'kier, Ki-Ham was blunt and frank; he could easily express his feelings and was not bothered by whether he was being insulting. This came from the high level of self-confidence that he possessed. Unlike Zula'kier, whose self-confidence would demonstrate itself as assertiveness, Ki-Ham's self-confidence would exhibit itself as aggressiveness.

Those who managed to tolerate him for a little while would find the privilege to know and understand Ki-Ham more and would soon discover that he really didn't mean to offend anyone. He just had a need to express himself, even though it meant arguing for a vain idea. Fortunately, he was very good at apologizing.

* * *

One dark afternoon, Ki-Ham and Zula'kier met in an alley in Lower Hay'at. One was walking south down the alley, and the other was walking north. They reached each other in the middle of the alley. As they reached each other, the first thing they noticed was how different they were. Their differences were obvious to each other. Despite that, Ki-Ham and Zula'kier immediately forged a strong friendship based on mutual respect and tolerance. They came to understand each other and enjoy each other's company. From that moment on, they would spend every second of their free time together, discussing everything from politics of the island to technology, medicine, and art. They gave each other the opportunity to learn from one another.

These two were not too vain to accept that they even enjoyed some innocent gossip behind the elders' backs. Hay'aties have insatiable appetites for gossip. Many simply cannot avoid being influenced by the opportunity to discuss a rumor. As much as they may pride themselves on their profoundness, it becomes very difficult at times not to be tempted, for occasionally the environment exerts a subtle influence on the good citizens of the oval-shaped island to indulge in gossip. At any rate, one would consider gossip a cultural trait. Every mode of entertainment on the island, from the early years of citizens' childhoods, teaches them that gossip is an acceptable form of passing time.

6 — Ki-Ham and Zula'kier

One hot and steamy afternoon, Ki-Ham was running toward Zula'kier's home. He was incredibly distressed. He had to stop a few times on his way. He would get out of breath and need to use both hands to catch his breath and put it back in his lungs. It was actually a fairly difficult and stressful exercise, considering that he was in a great hurry to get to Zula'kier's house. Every time he stopped to catch his breath, he would feel even more stressed. It was really a moment of relief when he finally arrived at his friend's home — and perfect timing as well. Ki-Ham arrived as Zula'kier was leaving. Zula'kier didn't look as if he was in a hurry, so Ki-Ham didn't mind stopping him.

"Have you heard? Have you heard what they are doing in the upper side?" Ki-Ham yelled, holding his heart with both hands.

"Forget that," said an excited Zula'kier. "Check this out."

Zula'kier had an apple in one hand and a piece of paper in the other. The piece of paper was a handwritten letter. Someone must have sent him a letter, probably from the upper side. An acquaintance? A relative, maybe? The handwriting on the paper was not very legible. Zula'kier kept waving the letter in the air, and that made it even more difficult for anyone to see what was written on it. Ki-Ham felt that Zula'kier didn't want anyone to see how bad the handwriting was. But he soon realized that Zula'kier was afraid that the words on the paper would run away, and he was waving the paper to make sure the words wouldn't find a strong footing so that they could walk off the paper and leave.

"Upper Hay'at is developing a product that can open the sky." Zula'kier chuckled.

"Oh, that is not really good news," Ki-Ham said, looking at the apple in Zula'kier's hand. "I heard from good authority that they are also experimenting with some new weaponry. That is what I wanted to tell you. They are fanatics. If they get their hands on something this dangerous, only gods know what they might do next; they may even try it on Lower Hay'at. That would physically and morally devastate both cities." Ki-Ham had problems containing his feelings.

"And it frightens you to think about death, doesn't it?" Zula'kier said mockingly.

"No, not really. I just don't want to die only because someone decides to try the destructive power of what has been created," Ki-Ham said, sitting down in a chair outside of Zula'kier's home. "I have no specific idea what we should do, how to prepare."

"That's not the point," said Zula'kier. "The point is that soon all will know that we will have a way to see whether there is anything outside or not."

Ki-Ham rested his forehead on his knee, staying in that position for a while. He was still out of breath. Then he moved his head up toward Zula'kier and slowly said, "Can I ask you a question?"

"Sure. Shoot."

"Tell me, how many gods do you think exist?"

"This is sacrilege, isn't it?" Zula'kier said with a smile.

It was crystal clear to Ki-Ham that Zula'kier hadn't liked the question; he was just trying to tolerate his friend.

"Let me rephrase it," Ki-Ham said in haste. The error

of his question was far too evident, and he knew that he had to tactfully fix his own mistake. "Do you think there is any difference between our gods as Lower Hay'aties and those of the Upper Hay'aties?"

"What do you mean?"

"Well, do you think that we all serve the same gods, or do you think that we serve different gods?"

"You are not making any sense. Of course we all serve the same gods."

Zula'kier invited his friend into his house. A couple of minutes later, they were both settled down on opposite sides of Zula'kier's worktable. Zula'kier put the apple that he had in his hand down on the table and then neatly folded the letter and gently put it on the table so that the writings on the paper remained tucked away, without any possibility of escaping.

"We are all part of the same society, the upper and lower. It should not matter," said Ki-Ham. "Our gods are the same. We came from the same place. We are the same. Let's discuss a hypothetical situation." He picked up two pens from the table and then put them next to each other. "Pen number one is a zealous Upper Hay'ati, born in an ancient city with a rich culture. It believes in the gods and the philosophy of life as it was written for the good citizens of the city. This pen knows that gods have protected the citizens of the city of Hay'at forever and will continue to do so as long as the universe exists."

He paused for a second and looked at Zula'kier, who clearly did not like where this conversation was going; after all, Zula'kier was from the upper side and Ki-Ham felt that the discussion was going in the direction that an upper sider might find offensive and degrading.

"Pen number two is a good Lower Hay'ati. This pen too believes that gods have been protecting the citizens of the city. This pen seriously accepts the fact that the creation of the lower side was the will of the gods. Like any good lower sider, this pen believes in the evolution of rules. It believes that gods gave us the rules but also gave us the power to change and help the rules evolve as our society evolves. Infants become toddlers; toddlers become kids and then teenagers. Societies too grow; so do rules and ideas. This second pen wants to see that ideas will grow and flourish and that other citizens won't follow a rule just because the society has been following that rule forever. This pen believes so much in the freedom of ideas that it is even willing to offer its life force."

"So far it is a good description of how the lower siders and the upper siders see the universe," Zula'kier said skeptically. He was still unsure where this discussion was going.

"To pen number one, the very existence of Hay'at depends on following what has been in their society for thousands of years, and these zealot citizens were shocked and disappointed at the mere idea of having Lower Hay'at created. What do you think these shocked and disappointed citizens dream every night of doing? Well, it is probably not very difficult to speculate. Let me propose an idea: they feel like destroying the lower side. The want to see the world unchanged. To them, we are the evil incarnate, the very personification of the worst thing that could have happened to the city of Hay'at. They would want to set out on a crusade to demolish the very idea of Lower Hay'at."

"Right." Zula'kier nodded.

"So a war breaks out. Pen one kills as many Lower Hay'aties as he can; he is serving his idea. His family and friends are proud of him, he has a lover back home praying for his safe return, and he feels the burden of the huge responsibility he is carrying on his shoulders. So he tries not to disappoint his fellow pens. Pen two also stays loyal to his idea. Do not get me wrong. Pen two has his own ideas, his own faith; when his faith is threatened, he will stand up for what he believes in, and he fights for his idea. He wants to serve his gods to the best of his abilities, and if this means making huge sacrifices and dying in the process, so be it. Right?" Ki-Ham looked at Zula'kier, who was listening carefully.

"Now somewhere along the way, the two pens have forgotten that they came from the same place, that their gods were actually the same gods. Eventually they both get killed. Who knows? They might have even killed each another. Pen one injures pen two," Ki-Ham said, playing with the pens and pretending as though they were fighting. "As pen two is falling down, he throws his spear, which hits pen one directly in the heart. Wow!" He threw the pens on the desk with a dramatic movement.

"They are on the ground among hundreds or even thousands of injured and dying Lower and Upper Hay'aties, staring at each other as they get ready to travel to the other world and to be with our kind and omnipotent gods. Now, my dear friend, tell me, what is the reward for someone who chooses to suffer in such a way in order for his idea to prevail?" Ki-Ham asked with a smile.

"The reward, of course, is that the ideas will prevail," Zula'kier answered indifferently.

"And as for our two good and nice pens, give me a reason why both ideas should prevail."

"Come again?" Zula'kier asked, shocked.

"It is very simple; we live in a binary world: black and white, day and night, good and evil. You just said the reward is that the idea will prevail, but only one of the two ideas should be right. If we are fighting, then only one idea should prevail. Should it not? One of the two ideas is evil, and the other one is good. One idea should prevail. But both ideas have originated from the same place. Logically, they are rooted in the same historical belief system. If one is evil, then logically the other one will become evil as well." Ki-Ham was getting more and more excited. "For crying out loud, it is not that complicated; you are right. Both ideas should prevail. Both ideas will be either good or evil."

"I guess you are right, under the circumstance—"

"Circumstance, schircumstance—don't justify it. It is very simple," Ki-Ham said, interrupting Zula'kier.

"Where is this conversation going?" Zula'kier asked impatiently.

"Well, the two pens are now dead. They are living with the gods in the other world. Pens one and two, who were mortal enemies not a minute ago, are now standing together. Remember, both served the same gods. They fought for their ideas, died for their ideas. So they are with our gods, rewarded for their sacrifices, looking through the great vase of the gods. They look at us, the pitiful people who are still fighting in vain." Ki-Ham gasped. "They were enemies, but now they are in a neutral place where hatred doesn't have any meaning, and they possess the power to look down at us—*on* us—and see the error of our way of life. They both are rewarded, meaning they both were right, and they killed each other for no reason. They were both tools in the hands of power-thirsty elders who wanted to have more power, more control, and in their quest to control the livelihood of their fellow citizens, these 'trustworthy' elders from both sides violated the most sacred code."

"And what would be this sacred code that they have violated and apparently you are the only one who is aware of? Remember that an elder becomes an elder because he or she possesses the ancient knowledge of the city of Hay'at. They have the support of the gods, and they have been selected by the House of Representatives, and the members of the House of Representatives have been chosen by us, the people. Both sides of the city of Hay'at are structured and governed the same way." Zula'kier's ideology was taking over. This was part of his heritage. Regardless of how tolerant he was of the lower side's ideology, he would still side with his hometown.

"Look around you. There is order in everything; the universe goes on in an orderly fashion. You are a scientist. On the outside, we see order, and on the inside, the foundation of our universe is based on chaos."

"And?"

"The reason for this duality is simple: it is because the first rule of the universe is harmony and peace. If you want to be a part of the great existence of life, you will have to learn to be in harmony with the rest of the creative blocks of the world. It does not matter how chaotic the foundation of life is; on the outside, we need order. On the outside, we need peace and harmony among all the building blocks of life. That means peace and harmony among people, who are the building blocks of our two societies. Can you imagine how beautiful it would be if everybody could live in peace, tranquility, and harmony?"

"But what if you have to defend yourself?" asked Zula'kier.

"In many cases you should ignore the need to defend yourself, even give in before getting involved in any form of physical engagement."

"You surely don't mean that. That would mean that if someone were to attack you, you would just sit back and be a spectator while they attack you, kill you, and seize your land and the rest of your livelihood," said a disgusted Zula'kier. "Do you honestly believe that? How could you even think like that? Do you believe if you ignored them, you could outgrow them in the long run?" Zula'kier said sarcastically.

"This is far more complicated than what you just articulated. But in short, yes. Someone has to be the bigger person; someone has to nip the idea of fighting in the bud before everything starts to get out of hand."

"Do you even hear yourself?" Zula'kier gasped.

"I know that years of hatred cannot be stopped overnight. The thirst for power and the desire to rule the universe have been the ultimate purposes and goals in life for many men. The city of Hay'at now has grown, and we will see more of those who desire the past." Ki-Ham paused for a second and then continued. "Someone has to step up. Someone has to make the decision to stop this before it gets out of hand."

"So you want a nation to be like grass, *moving* in response to the gust of wind."

"Not until the end of time—only for a limited time. War breeds war; peace breeds peace. We just need to find the determination, perseverance, and will to achieve peace." Ki-Ham was panting now. "What would you propose: to kill other innocent people and then take revenge for the innocent people who have been killed? When is this mess going to end?"

"If that is how everybody feels, how do you propose to change the very nature of us? Do you want to change the nature of all Hay'aties from the lower and the upper sides?" Zula'kier said sarcastically.

"You know better." Ki-Ham shrugged. "No matter how insignificant one is or one's actions might seem, one can still make a deep impression on the course of the universe."

Ki-Ham was right. Even a creature as insignificant as a tiny butterfly has the power to cause a hurricane to change the course of history as long as the small butterfly has the will. To make such a massive change, it only needs to flutter its wings. That is all it takes.

7—Why Are We Fighting Anyway?

Zula'kier looked perplexed. Ki-Ham had him puzzled. He had this effect on people; he would mix up different subjects and ideas together as he talked. Then he would jump from one subject to another and back; his approach would confuse even the most focused and the smartest Hay'ati. Ki-Ham wasn't the type of person who would spend time preparing any speeches; he'd make up and build his premise as he talked. His remarks, as they were now, were generally off the cuff. At some point one would even recognize that Ki-Ham was indeed thinking out loud, as it were.

He always began with some basic and simple idea, an opinion he had about a subject. He had the objective defined in his head and would build the story around the objective. The challenge, however, was that since he hadn't worked out the idea in detail in his head before, the delivery of the idea would falter, and the idea, at some point, would be confusing and difficult to fathom.

Any idea has to come out eventually to get challenged, to grow, and to develop into a powerful notion. After all, a powerful idea transfers some of its power and strength to one who challenges it.[4] Ideas are like the humans who create them. Ideas are born, and then they go through the human life cycle of infancy and upward until they eventually die.

---

[4] Marcel Proust, *Within a Budding Grove Volume 1,* trans. C. K. Scott Moncrieff (London: Chatto & Windus, 1923), 191.

What is an *idea* anyway? Is it not, in fact, the result of questioning what seems to be the currently accepted fact? Great ideas start off with questioning what has been accepted as the norm, the convention, or even the truth. They start out as innocent and simple inquiries; in the long run, some of them evolve into the greatest achievements.

As Leon Trotsky put it, ideas that enter the mind under fire remain there securely and forever.[5] The more strenuous the circumstance of the birth of an idea is, the more prominent the idea will be. Ideas have to be put into practice, or soon they'll become stale. Staleness is the beginning of the end for an idea. That is how an idea will go downhill and will eventually go out of existence.

At first a new notion sounds lovely; it is attractive and preoccupies the mind of its creator at all times. But there is always a fork in the road. Some powerful authors decide to share the infant ideas they have created. On the other hand, some other authors decide to meditate on the ideas, to wait before they act on them or share them. Hesitation in expressing what once seemed like an exquisite idea will result in converting it into a cold and exhausting reality. The question is not whether you have any ideas of your own. Everyone has ideas. Some even have the greatest ideas in the world. The question is when the idea is born in one's head, is one ready and brave enough to express the idea, share it, and, above all, stand by it?

"Where are you?" asked a smiling Ki-Ham.

"You got me confused," said Zula'kier. "I'm not following; I don't know what you are really trying to convey. Do you want people to be living peacefully together by bowing to the bullies who push them around?"

"You got it," Ki-Ham said ironically.

---

[5] Leon Trotsky, *My Life* (1930; repr., New York: Dover, 2007), 432.

"But what is the point of life if one ends up living a meaningless existence, a life that is under strain, stress, and all forms of physical and mental, not to mention spiritual, pressure and duress? Even abjection has its limit. Real men would rather die than live in perdition," Zula'kier said passionately. "I just have to ask: don't you credit those who fight for what they believe? Do you not see any value in how they live their lives?"

"*Real men*, you say?" said Ki-Ham. "Who are these *real men*? Who has the right to judge people and label some of them as real? If some are labeled as real, then it stands to reason that there must be those who should be labeled as unreal. Also, the more important question is: who is more real, one who stands by one's ideas, fights for one's beliefs, and is even willing to die for them, or one who, for the sake of one's family, is willing to live under any condition obsequiously just so one's family survives and flourishes, regardless of what might happen to one's ideas and beliefs?"

"I admire both."

"For one thing, you have no basis to prove whether the principles of the first person are worth dying for even if they are correct. You'll never know if the first person had been deceived," Ki-Ham said with an ominous smile. "We live in Lower Hay'at. We believe in what the lower side stands for. And yet who is to say that we are right? Who is to say that what we believe is right and that we should fight and die for it? All I can say is that we are more flexible than our counterparts; that is all."

All of a sudden, there was a pause—an ugly, painful silence. Zula'kier had his own special form of silence.

Some forms of silence are so subtle that it takes paramount attention, time, effort, and delicacy to learn their meanings. Some people have a special gift to manipulate silence to grant it a deep meaning; the silence they create is filled with wisdom and wit. There are those who spend most of their lives trying to uncover the meaning of such silences. There are scientists who watch and cherish every movement and form of body language to understand the true nature of the silence of its owner.

Zula'kier, being conservative, would go to great lengths to keep his family safe; being a true believer, he would advocate a belief system. Of course, he couldn't for sure decide on whether or not he would fight for the ideas that the upper side stood for, no matter how much he believed in them.

Ki-Ham could see the contradiction he had caused.

"I'm a theorist, aren't I?" said Ki-Ham.

Zula'kier nodded.

There was a pause. It was the sound of tiredness; it was sharp and displeasing. They were both in a prison with no way out. Ki-Ham was deep in his thoughts. He could remember the trace of a memory at the back of his mind, something that he had experienced.

8—His Memories, a Short Story by Ki-Ham

It is a day like any other day. From south to north, west to east, north to south, and east to west, men, women, and children awaken to the same old things. This day is a repetition of any other day, and people are so used to these days that they do not even recognize, and therefore do not care, that they are living a boring routine.

Ignorance is *not* an evil weed but bliss. It does *not* breed crime but success. Ignorance is a delightful concept that brings longevity, passion, and love. Never forgive anyone who wastes your time, clouds your mind, and makes you think, for he deserves nothing but hatred, exile, imprisonment, and death. Instead, seek who feeds your ignorance.

* * *

He is running, holding a child under his right arm while carrying something heavy with his left hand. He grew up in that field; however, he has no clue where he is going. He is running for his life. Although it is the mild season in the city of Hay'at, the weather is incredibly hot and humid. He will not think where he is going; he does not care that he just ran past the tree where he engraved his name. He can't remember his childhood. He doesn't see trees; he sees obstacles that he must avoid at all costs.

Survival—he must survive. He wants to survive even if all the men and women in this universe belittle him and call him a coward.

He dodges some folded branches. His left arm is in pain; his right arm is even worse. His biceps are numb. He is still not thinking; his mind is blank.

The kid celebrated his seventh birthday two months and four days ago. He is rather skinny, long-haired, and tanned, with a pair of big eyes that are terrified and quiet, yet very much alive. When his mouth is ajar, his half-broken front tooth can be seen. His head keeps jerking, and he feels like vomiting, but he will not. He wants to prove that he is strong.

The kid wants to survive and knows that survival depends on not causing any trouble—on staying quiet and waiting. He is too young to know how to think or what to think about. What is *thinking* anyway? He certainly doesn't know. What he knows is that he needs to be quiet and as motionless as a dead rat. He repeats that to himself. He *thinks* it.

The man is still running as though the devil himself is chasing him. All of a sudden, he stops. He notices something. What could that be? He does not even recognize the ruins where he used to play hide-and-seek. Instinctively, he goes toward the ruins. Not running vigorously but walking slowly, he enters a ramshackle room in the middle of the ruins, puts the kid on the ground, and collapses on the floor, stretching his arms. He sighs. He is tired. He feels how dry his mouth is. His heart is racing. His hands and knees are trembling.

The kid sits by the front wall, leans back, and gathers his legs in to his stomach; he has never been so scared in his entire life, not even when he broke the thousand-year-old family medallion and his mother threatened to kill him. Not even when his father got drunk and hit him, broke his tooth, and left him alone to die, something that would have happened had his uncle not found him. No, this time it is different. It is not serious; as a matter of fact, it seems unreal. It is just different. And the difference makes it a horrifying experience. How much he wants to go to sleep and wake up in the warm bosom of his mother, listening to her kind words; those nice words would make him feel strong and safe again. But she is away; she is sleeping in the other world now.

* * *

There are abrupt, sharp sounds off to...everywhere. A short, hoarse cry comes from the distance, the other side of the world. Someone else died. But does it really matter? There are people living all over the universe; there are thousands of fathers, brothers, and sons. One, ten, or a hundred less—as long as it is not him, or his father, or his son, it will not make any difference to him. Furthermore, people die of natural causes every day; there is no stop to death. The god of gods commissioned the god of death to keep the population of the universe balanced. He said everything needed to be in moderation, even the population of the city of Hay'at. The gods gave this city to the people to live in it, and they leave it in peace so long as the people understand and believe in moderation. It took years, but eventually the citizens have learned how to reduce the population of their universe. They discovered that they can kill one other.

He gets up. He needs to do something. He is not alone; he has to take care of the kid. *Responsibility* is the greatest and deepest word that has ever been created. He now feels the burden of *responsibility*.

He is ready to be responsible for someone else; he cares for his cousin, who came by his house exactly three hours, twenty-one minutes, and ten seconds ago. The cousin came with a grand responsibility to pass on to him. The kid is family, is vulnerable, and is frightened. He doesn't know how, but he knows that he has to take care of the kid, support him, and be the pillar he needs right now to ensure that the kid will survive this ordeal. He *will* do whatever is in his power.

Four hours, sixteen minutes, and eleven seconds— that is all the time that the two of them have shared in this universe. This is not a long history to share. Yet they are going to share only another 208 seconds together.

9—The Apple

All of a sudden, Ki-Ham burst out with, "They must be looking unhappily back at me from the land of the gods! All the old and dead elders, I mean."

Zula'kier did not look very happy at all. But his bewilderment was still there.

Zula'kier collected himself and asked a very simple question: "What are you asking me?" His feelings and his thoughts were heating up. "There is nothing anybody could possibly do."

"But there is, my good friend," Ki-Ham said with a Cheshire-cat grin. "Do you want to know what the solution is? Just don't think this way anymore. Tell your friends and anybody you know to change the way they think. Try to spread the word of tolerance, friendship, harmony, and peace. Even if you manage to change the way *one* person reflects, senses, and perceives, we have won; we'll be on our way to a better world. Don't you think so?"

Zula'kier didn't answer. He was skeptical, and Ki-Ham could smell his skepticism.

"You think I am crazy; you think I am a delusional dreamer, don't you?"

"Not at all," Zula'kier responded thoughtfully.

"Someone needs to stop fighting. It takes only one person—one person to help one other person, to help another person live longer or be safer," Ki-Ham commented. "I guess it's high time we considered humankind before our ideals." Ki-Ham had become very serious now.

Ki-Ham got up and started pacing up and down. "Have you ever thought that every bad person is the brother, son, father, mother, or daughter of a good person? You see, I'm the worst person, but when I die, when I'm gone, my good, kind, and caring parents will suffer. There is another aspect to this as well; if the devastation happens, if the worst case comes true, there will be a horrifying outcome. The defeated side will be destroyed—will be gone. The victorious, on the other hand, will not be in any better shape."

Ki-Ham paused for a second or two before he continued. "The universe will be shattered; the champions will be in the worst state of affairs. Everywhere there will be fire and despair. Homes will be filled with mothers crying for their dead sons and husbands. It doesn't matter who they were; the truth is that they are dead. They are gone, and their dependents are left alone. Remember that all the lower siders have relatives, close or distant, in the upper side. We are all somehow related."

"You see, Ki-Ham, you have your idea, and I have mine. It should not bother you; it is just an idea. Why are you trying so hard to make me believe you?"

"It is not that I want you to believe in me or see the world from my point of view. I just want you to try to understand me; that's all."

The apple was still on the table. Zula'kier picked it up and asked Ki-Ham whether he'd like to have some.

"Sure."

"Catch," Zula'kier said, throwing the apple toward him. Ki-Ham caught it in midair and looked at it; it was reddish and shining. He could see his face in it. He took a bite. It was sweet. Ki-Ham chewed on it slowly, savoring every bit. He kept on chewing for a while before he finally swallowed it down.

Part 3

I Had Been Considering Buying a Parrot

10—I Had Been Considering Buying a Parrot

It was quite some time before the news of the disappearance of Dr. J. Burgess reached his son, at which point Dr. K. decided to share an idea with his sister. Dr. Burgess senior was traveling, and that was all his children knew about his whereabouts. Yet there was a certain queasiness that Dr. K. Burgess was experiencing, and to overcome that feeling, he had decided to keep busy. He had gone back to an old idea that he had had since his childhood. He wanted to share that with his sister. He was not looking for any support, judgment, or even acknowledgment. He only wanted to share his idea with another human being.

Many a time we face a complex situation in life. Deep down we know that we have the solution to it within us, yet we don't know where the solution might be hiding. That is when we feel that we should share the idea with someone. Some of us who are fortunate enough to have a confidant discuss the different aspects of what has heavily occupied our minds, while our confidant only listens. As we talk and our listener listens (nonjudgmentally, of course), a miracle happens. The solutions are awakened, leave their hiding places, and comes to the surface of our stomachs. We recognize the solution as what it is, reach for it, and pick it up to use it.

Sometimes we have already found the solution to our outstanding challenge, and still we desire the nonjudgmental ears of our confidant.

That was why Dr. K. needed to talk to his sister. He

knew what the problem was; he also knew what he wanted to do. Still, he went to see his sister, and after the usual pleasantries, he started.

"I have been considering buying a parrot for a long time because everybody I know has at least one; some even have more than one. I've never managed to fathom how they could justify investing so much money in a parrot, for having a parrot is an expensive business. First, it is the money one needs to spend to purchase the parrot. Then comes the cost to feed and take care of one's parrot. Parrots eat quite a bit, and they get sick quite often. The medication is often expensive. There is also the issue of selecting what sort of parrot to purchase. There are different species and different breeds of parrots. Some eat less and live longer, yet they are expensive to buy; some, on the other hand, are cheaper to buy, yet they require more food to eat, and their life expectancy is limited to a few years.

"As though these expenses were not enough to discourage a potential buyer, there is another expensive matter anyone should consider before buying a parrot: the insurance. I never liked the insurance industry; insurance companies are willing to insure anything these days, and since parrot-buying has become a major business nowadays, it seems to me that a major part of the income of insurance companies is from insuring parrots. Fortunately, insuring a parrot is not required by law, but I don't know anyone who owns an uninsured parrot.

"Some people even go to great lengths to purchase the best insurance for their parrots from other countries, while they will not buy life insurance for themselves at all. It seems that whether or not they provide for their nearest and dearest in case of their demise is of little importance to them. What is important to them is being able to recover the loss of their investment so they can almost immediately replace their parrot, preferably with another bird that looks the same as the already deceased one to alleviate the melancholy that the death of a parrot causes. Insuring parrots is becoming a standard practice in most countries, and the insurance industry, over the years, has learned that people would pay anything to make sure their beloved parrots are fully insured. It has become a matter of prestige for the esteemed bird owners.

"But there are complexities with the insurance premiums. The younger a parrot is, the higher the premium the owner will have to pay, for a younger parrot is more expensive and more difficult to replace. The premium will be higher if this is the owner's first bird, too; in this case, the friendly insurance company will make the poor parrot owner pay through his nose. At the same time, the insurance industry never fails to keep increasing the premium.

"I couldn't make up my mind for a long time about buying a parrot. As a matter of fact, I had considered buying a parrot before; once I was even about to buy a very expensive species, but having done extensive research, I had arrived at the conclusion that I didn't need to buy one. At the time, I had thought that I would never need to buy such a luxurious commodity. That was when I had lost a lot of money in my first investment venture; you surely remember that. I was living a mediocre life at the time, which did not require a parrot.

"Nonetheless, I would go to work and come back home thinking about my colleagues and neighbors and their parrots. Needless to say, I would feel ashamed that I didn't have a parrot of my own. I would borrow some of my friends' parrots at times only to show off. I would explain, as I just did, that purchasing a parrot is complicated. But the reality was that the research and calculations I had done and even the insurance story were all only lame excuses for me not to buy a parrot. I wasn't really worried about the money. I could always borrow the money from our father to pay for all the expenses of a parrot, including the insurance premium. There was yet another reason for my decision—or rather, my indecision—at the time. My procrastination was rooted in a different garden.

"Many years before, I was taking care of a parrot; it was before you were born. I had to give it up. The parrot, as a matter of fact, was not mine; it was our father's, and when I was away on a school trip, Father decided it was time to sell the parrot, or to 'get rid of the bird,' as he had put it, although not very delicately. I was never part of any parrot support group. I never believed that parrots had feelings and that we humans could hurt their feelings. Still, I never talked so inconsiderately about anything that was part of our family.

"That parrot was part of our everyday lives for three years. Our dad had bought it for our mother, but our mother decided that she didn't want to have a parrot for herself, so our father gave the parrot to me. I never had to do anything for the parrot except for the occasional feeding. Although the parrot was rather an old bird, and more often than not it had to be taken to the vet, I was very comfortable with the creature. In fact, Father would take care of its needs entirely. After we 'got rid of the bird,' I decided I didn't need a parrot anymore. Not having a parrot for many years, I wasn't used to having one anymore.

"The commitment of having a parrot has powerful hands and muscles. It could grab someone by the collar and not let one move. Although people from any age could have parrots, and there are even some parrot owners as young as ten, and they take care of their birds beautifully, I was, until very recently, still terrified of buying one for myself and changing my lifestyle accordingly. What if the parrot got sick, especially on a freezing winter day? Then I'd have to take it to a vet. I wasn't so sure I could commit to all the responsibilities that came with the bird.

"Eventually, the time comes in everybody's lives when they have to purchase their own parrots. When the time came, I recognized it and decided that it was the right time for me to buy one. So I set off to find and buy a reliable, preferably talking, parrot. The first place I looked was the classified sections of the paper. I opened the paper and looked under the section 'Parrots for Sale.' There were pages on end in this section; I could never go through all those ads. I arbitrarily chose one ad and read it carefully. The ad I was looking at seemed to be about a very interesting and fine parrot. It didn't say what the price of the bird was, but it did say that the bird was from a low-eating breed. I, therefore, picked up the phone to call and talk to the owner of the parrot and to discuss the health, age, and price of the bird. I couldn't believe the nerve of the seller when he told me that it was an eight-year-old parrot. No self-respecting salesman would try to sell an eight-year-old parrot, and if I had bought the parrot, what would my friends have thought about me: that I was so cheap I couldn't invest a little more money to purchase a more reasonable and finer parrot?

"Other advertisements weren't any better; looking at a few, I gathered that the best way to find a good parrot would be to walk up to an actual shop and look at the merchandise they had to offer. I decided to go and look at some shops right away; knowing me, if I had put it off, I would have probably never bought my parrot. I picked up the directory, looked at the classified section under 'Parrots for Sale,' wrote down some addresses, and set off on the mission to find a good parrot. I was going to buy something not very expensive yet from a good breed, something that wouldn't eat a lot and was reliable enough that it wouldn't spend eight days a week at a vet.

"Yes, I am well aware there are only seven days in a week; you don't have to growl at me and correct me.

"Everybody knows the older a parrot is, the less expensive its insurance is. However, there are a few problems with old parrots: they tend to get sick, and they don't look quite as nice and interesting as younger parrots, and they die soon.

"The first shop I went to was closed, but I could look through its windows, and I clearly didn't like the parrots they had. The parrots mostly looked old; maybe I wasn't off to a good start. The second shop, Bird Bargain, was fantastic. They had a selection of *second-hand*, for lack of a better term, parrots, some as good as new. I immediately fell in love with one of them. It was as green as a cornfield from five thousand feet. Its beak was chipped, and that certainly was a put-off. The parrot's tag read that the bird was one year old. It was the kind of a parrot I could see myself with. It wasn't a talking parrot, but that didn't concern me at the time. I looked at the price tag, and I liked the price of the bird as well. It was well within my budget.

"The sales manager of the shop, a tall, blond woman in her early forties, looking disheveled and sitting behind her desk, was closing a deal with an old couple. The couple was trying to bring down the price of a five-year-old parrot. I looked around; I went through the aisles and looked at the different parrots they had. Some of the parrots were brand new and from very famous breeds. I even saw some other birds that I couldn't recognize running on the shop floor. I felt bad when I realized I didn't know the names of half of those types of birds. A young man walked toward me; his name tag read, 'Your Sales Representative, James.'

"'Can I help you, sir?' he said. I found his tone very polite and considerate.

"'Sure,' I replied. 'I'm looking for a parrot.'

"'What kind of a parrot are you looking to buy?' asked James. I immediately felt stupid. I knew what kind I was going to buy, but I had never thought I would have to explain it to someone else. I was facing the problem of articulating my demand. My thoughts were racing in my head, and I had difficulty trying to keep up with them. I took a deep breath to slow down the speed of my thoughts. It took me a few seconds, but I was again in control of my thoughts.

"'Nothing very spectacular,' I said. 'Not expensive, and not very cheap either. I don't want to spend every day at a vet. Preferably a bird that doesn't eat too much.' Somehow, magically, I had managed to communicate the type of bird I wanted to have.

"'Are you looking to buy a talking parrot?' asked James.

"'They are more expensive than the other kinds, aren't they?' I asked.

"'Oh, yes, absolutely, sir.' James was shocked that I had even dared to confirm such an obvious point. He hadn't realized that I was looking for my first parrot.

"'No, I don't think I want to buy a talking bird then,' I lied, looking at the price tag of the green parrot. The green parrot seemed to be perfect in every sense—except for its chipped beak and not being able to talk, of course, but neither bothered me at that point.

"'This parrot is one of our bestselling kinds. This one is one year old. I can assure you it is going to be very well within your budget.' It seemed that James had guessed my budget for buying a parrot. On the other side of the shop, the saleswoman, acting on her nature, was still trying to make her sale by making the old couple believe that they were getting a very good deal on the five-year-old parrot. I felt uncomfortable; even I could see that it was not a good deal, and I am by no means an expert in this field. I felt that the saleswoman was rather a dishonest person, and that made me trust the salespeople at this shop less.

"'We have the lowest prices at Bird Bargain,' said the saleswoman. 'No one can compete with us on price. Did I tell you about the warranty we offer on our birds? We guarantee that your parrot will not have any problem for six months after purchase. If you'd like, we can increase the guarantee to one year for only ten percent of the price of the bird.' In the end she not only sold them the parrot but made them believe it was their choice, and in the end, they were totally appreciative of the assistance and support that they received from her.

"As the old, happy couple was leaving the shop, James looked at me. 'Do you think you are going to buy a parrot today, sir?' He had smelled my hesitation.

"'Yes, I have made up my mind, and I know that I'm ready to buy a parrot today,' I said happily. I thought that it was going to be the first parrot that was entirely mine and that it was going to be great.

"'In this case, let me get my manager, and she will be able to help you with different species and breeds we have here,' said James. I nodded. The old couple had left, and the saleswoman was walking around the shop, looking at her birds, when James approached her. They talked for a minute or two, and then she walked toward me.

"'Hi. I'm Rita,' she said. 'I'm the sales manager here at Bird Bargain. How can I help you today, sir?' She was extremely polite.

"'I'm looking to buy a parrot,' I responded quickly. 'I like this breed,' I said, pointing at my green parrot.

"'Very nice choice,' Rita said encouragingly. 'This is a very popular breed and from a wonderful species too; this is one of our finest pieces of merchandise. Such merchandise never lasts long in a shop, you know.' She was heartening, but I wasn't the type of person who would get influenced by a salesperson easily. Nonetheless, there was something about the bird. I was standing in front of Rita, my back to the bird. As I was talking to Rita, I had a distinct feeling that the parrot was looking at me. I could feel the weight of its stare on my back; it was very warm.

"'Its beak is chipped,' I said.

"'Oh.' Rita looked indifferent. 'We can send the bird down to our vet shop; they will replace its beak and send it back to us. It will take only a couple of days.'

"I turned around and looked at the parrot's innocent eyes. They were heartwarming and had a meaningful influence. 'I can give you a down payment, and when it is ready, I'll come back and pick it up.' I had made a life-changing decision.

"'Good decision,' said Rita. 'I'll call you when it is back from the vet.'

"I paid Rita and left the shop. On my way back home, I couldn't think of anything else but the fact that I had just bought a parrot. Unsuccessfully, I tried to divert my attention from what I had done to the parrot's eyes. I kept pushing my imagination toward the parrot's innocent eyes, but with no use. By the time I got home, all my body was covered in a rash, and my skin had started to bleed. I went to the bathroom and looked at myself in the mirror. 'It wasn't a talking parrot,' I said to myself as I was looking at my bleeding face. I let my skin bleed, and I went straight to bed; I was feeling sick to my stomach. *It is not going to have its original beak; why did I buy this bird?* I managed not to think about my rash and the blood and to force myself to sleep.

"As I was sleeping, an aroma filled my bedroom—an aroma of uncertainty about what I had done. In my sleep, I chose to ignore the aroma; I knew that I would get used to it very soon. Then the phone rang, which made me wake up with a start. My heart started pounding, which made my bleeding even worse. I reached for the phone and picked it up. It was difficult to focus on the voice I was hearing in the receiver of the phone; my heart was still racing. It was an old friend on the other side of the line telling me that he had found a six-month-old parrot from a rare African breed for a very good price. It was a talking bird. I wasn't bleeding anymore.

"I got up and went to drink a glass of water. On my way to the kitchen, I looked at my face in the mirror; the rash was gone too. *I have to get my down payment back from Rita tomorrow. I have to cancel my purchase*, I told myself, and again I felt my heart racing as I started to review how I would go the shop, what I would tell Rita, and how I would get my money back. I was a bit nervous that Rita may not accept it, but then I told myself that the shop had a return policy, and I hadn't even taken the bird home yet, so she should be fine with canceling the purchase and paying me back my down payment. I was very unhappy with myself that I had suggested to leave a down payment. Why had I done that?

"The next day after work, I went to see Rita. I had called my friend and confirmed that I was going to buy the parrot he had found for me. My friend was very experienced as far as parrots were concerned. He hardly ever took his parrots to a vet—and he had three parrots, one of which was from a very special breed. He would take care of the parrots as much as he could without taking them to a vet. I always wondered about how much money he spent to insure his parrots.

"When I entered the shop, Rita was on the phone; she offered me a seat. I was still worried that she might not agree to return my down payment. I remembered how she had handled the old couple the day before, and that made me feel even more worried. When her phone call was over, two hundred and eleven seconds later—which felt like an eternity—she turned to me and said, 'You must be here to have one last look at your parrot before we send it to the vet.' She was smiling. I remembered that I didn't like her the previous day. I liked her even less now.

"'Actually, I have decided to cancel my purchase,' I said sheepishly.

"'Why?' She didn't sound happy at all.

"'Well, a friend of mine has found me a younger talking parrot, and I think I'm going with that one.'

"'You were looking for a talking parrot?' she asked, shocked. 'If you wanted to buy a talking parrot, why did you choose that bird? I'm confused; I don't understand why you chose that parrot while you knew you wanted a talking bird.'

"'I didn't want to buy a talking parrot, but when I went home last night and talked to my wife, she said that she would prefer a talking parrot.'

"Well, of course I am not married, but Rita didn't have to know that. Pretending to be married was the perfect technique, which I had used before; when I was doing my road test for my driver's license, I failed to stop at a stop sign. I thought that the examiner, sitting in the passenger seat, would definitely fail me, so I said, 'Oh, my wife is going to kill me.' To my amazement, the examiner laughed and did not fail me. So I wanted to use the help of my imaginary wife again.

"Rita opened the top drawer of her desk and took out the money I had given her the last night. 'We have some new species coming in next week,' she said, handing me back the money. 'They are all talking birds and generally very young, some even less than six months old. Would you like me to let you know when they arrive? If you wait until next week, I'm sure we can find you a better parrot than what your friend has found you—and cheaper too.'

"'Really?' I asked. 'I would love that. I'm in no hurry. I will definitely wait until next week to see your new birds.' I have no idea why I was not being honest. Maybe I was just afraid of what she might say. I know I should not have cared about that. I realized it as soon as I said it.

"After I left Bird Bargain, I went to a different store. This store had a massive collection of parrots with no one to ask me any questions or try to help me. I walked around and picked up a white talking parrot. It had the most piercing eyes. I paid for it and took it home with me. It has been over a week that I have been living with this amazing creature. Having such a beautiful creature in one's life is amazingly fulfilling. My friend is probably still waiting for me to go and buy the parrot he found for me. I'm sure he won't mind that I changed my mind.

"This morning I received an invitation from Rita to go and see her new parrots; apparently, the collection of birds that she was talking about has arrived. The invitation said that the birds are in various colors. Somehow I have to let her know that I am no longer in the market for a parrot. I am not sure if I need to explain and tell her that I am now the proud owner of a white talking parrot. Maybe I just ignore her. Do you think I should ignore her?"

At this point Dr. K. Burgess stopped, probably waiting for an answer.

His sister, peering into his eyes, took a deep breath. "Have you heard anything from our father?" she asked.

Part 4

Immortality

11 — Immortality

Ki-Ham looked at the old man and said, "I don't know whether you really want to hear the story yet another time — and this time from me — and to be honest, I don't care. There. I said it. I don't care. You see, no one ever listened to my side of the story. They all pretended to listen; they looked like they were all ears, but it was so obvious that they were all daydreaming as I was telling them the whole thing.

"Everything was predetermined. I don't know if that shocked me. Throughout my life I have been zigzagging between believing in free will and rejecting it altogether. I do not know what I believe in now. The actions of those folks seemed predetermined. All I see these days is predetermined actions. Then again, these actions are really the consequence of the actions that I took on my own. So maybe they are not really predetermined. Maybe free will does exist. Or maybe it does not exist. I don't know; I don't know anything anymore, and I do not care. I am beyond life and death now. I have achieved what I wanted. It has been a great success, and therefore I don't care what others think about me.

"Anyway, I never told anyone my story from the very beginning; neither did I ever try to impress anyone with the amazing facts that I had. Instead, I just conveyed the main sets of information, the basic facts. Except for occasional nods and a few smiles, I didn't get much out of anyone about my story; I could see right through everyone while I was acting as their storyteller, and that was what I was to my audience: just a storyteller. They tried to be polite, and my audience was the politest of them all. Again, like I said, I don't care.

"Where was I? You see, since my wife left me, between this, that, and the other, I have occasional lapses in memory; my mind just wanders off, and I easily forget what I was saying or doing. Huh? I was telling you about my side of the story? Oh, yes, I remember now.

"You know Zula'kier, don't you? What am I saying? Who doesn't know him? Since he reached immortality, his name has been on the tips of everybody's tongues. Everywhere you look, you can see people talking about him. As you can imagine, I haven't had the chance to see it myself, but I'm pretty sure there are posters and pictures of him all over Lower Hay'at. Actually, you can tell me. Aren't there any pictures of him all across the city? No? Are you sure? That can't be true. I don't believe it. The man reaches the highest level of existence, the level that everybody has been trying to reach, and now that he has managed, there are no pictures of him anywhere? But I'm positive he is famous anyway; isn't he? There you go; so he is famous after all. Maybe they didn't put his picture up because he is just so famous that no one needs to see a picture of him.

"I have to stop before I start going off at a tangent again. You see, I never prepared for any lectures or speeches. I had the gift of gab; I could build up a story whenever I needed to discuss a subject, and I always managed to communicate everything clearly—and of course I could get people confused whenever I wanted to get them confused. That was my power. I guess I have the right to be proud of myself. The good thing is that I remember I was telling you about Zula'kier.

"Well, let me start by telling you that Zula'kier was my best friend; I knew him for a long time. Shocked, eh? I knew it. No one even suspected that he was a friend of mine. As a matter of fact, Zula'kier and I were inseparable for as long as he was living in the lower side; he was at my wedding. I bet this is not a known fact either. Of course, why would anyone care, right? He was one of only two people at my wedding, so it did matter — at least to me.

"I have to confess that I'm a bit disappointed; I was hoping my name would follow his in more ways than one. What do you know? He becomes immortal and famous, and I'm just the loser I have always been. I appreciate you trying to make me feel better, yet in all honesty, I have to say it is too late for that, and I'm sure you know it is late too. What can I say? Anyhow, loser or not, I am on my way to immortality myself, so, again, I do not care about anything.

"Zula'kier was a strong personality even as a young man, always trying to leave an impression. He was a conservative, like most of the upper siders. The most important thing I remember about him is that he was obsessed with immortality. Some people are obsessed with progress, some with making money, some with becoming powerful; they all understand and accept that they all will die one day. They don't even try to challenge this fact; they accept it and focus on what they can control. Yet once in a blue moon, someone brave enough comes along and calls this reality into question — someone who understands that reality is relative, and as a matter of fact, everything is relative.

"Zula'kier was such a person; he knew he could do anything if he decided. The proof of this notion was the fact that he could have any woman he wanted, and one of them happened to be my wife. There. I said it. Now I'm sure this is what everyone knows about me and Zula'kier; to them that's what really matters: 'Oh, that guy's wife ran away with Zula'kier,' and everything that they would normally say. What I don't understand is the insatiable appetite for jumping the gun, judging others, and even worse, gossiping.

"Yes, I don't understand the need, but I can feel the need myself. I would enjoy talking about people behind their backs as much as the next guy; the more well-known the person is, the sweeter the gossip becomes. This seems to be a normal characteristic of us Hay'aties, whether we are from Upper or Lower Hay'at. We live in a small city; I mean the lower side is fairly small compared to the upper side. Many of us know one other. That makes the gossip interesting—you know, juicy. In this hodgepodge of life, we need our personal mode of entertainment, and when you look really closely, you'll see that every form of entertainment stems from gossip. Hm...maybe it is a disease, you know; maybe we are all infected by a virus.

"Oh, yes, I'm wandering away again; at least I'm lucid, eh? And I bring a smile to your face. You don't need to hide it; I can see it.

"As I was saying, my wife and Zula'kier had an affair. I can't really tell you when it started; what I can tell you is that once during a heated argument, just before my wife left me, she told me that they had slept together on the day we got married. No, you are right; it was probably something she said just to get on my last nerve. She just wanted to hurt me. Believe me; it worked. It hit me so hard that I fell and broke the back of my skull. Oh, it still hurts. Then again, she always knew how to hit me with her words. My wife became yet another of Zula'kier's lovers until he got tired of her and kicked her out.

"You are wondering if I saw my wife again. As a matter of fact, I did. I was shopping one day when I saw her. I couldn't muster up enough courage to go forward and say anything to her. Not that she was scary; I just couldn't do it.

Besides, I didn't have much to say to her. Between you and me, I did want to go to her and tell her that she got what she deserved. I wanted to see her unhappy. For once I wanted to use my words to hurt her. I know it sounds stupid, but her unhappiness would have made me very happy. I didn't do it. I couldn't bring myself to do it.

"Well, that's what really happened, and now you know it.

"We continued to walk our separate ways. Although it made me really mad that my wife ran off with Zula'kier, when Zula'kier came back to use my help, I wasn't thinking about the incident that had shattered my life. No, sir. When he came for my help, he was again my old friend, and I was there to help him. I don't know why it is so difficult for everyone to understand and accept what I did; I did it for the sake of our friendship and the immense respect I had for my dear and old friend. I told you about Zula'kier's obsession with immortality; like the old man said, when there is a will, there is a way. He had set his mind to it and finally did it. He must have spent many nights just dreaming about it until he managed to find what he was looking for. I have the utmost respect for his perseverance.

"I shall never forget that night as long as I live in this body—which, by the way, is going to be a short period of time, apparently. Once I become immortal, I will no longer need this body. I will no longer care about any such childish incidents anyway.

"It was a damp and humid night. I was at home. I'm not going to lie to you; I was drunk when he knocked on my door.

"What do you mean when you say 'as always'? It is not like I'm always drunk. Oh, well, it is like you can see through me. Yes, recently I have been drunk, mostly since she left me and I lost my job.

"Anyhow, I opened the door, and there he was, standing in wet clothes like a drowned rat. It was a damp and humid night. I'll be honest; I had always wanted to see him alone with a good opportunity to strangle him and watch him jerk, suffer, and die. And when he showed up at my door, for a fraction of a second, I thought about doing it, too. But only for a fraction of a second. The thought was soon gone. I am not—*was* not into revenge. Revenge is meaningless.

"It was not long until I discovered why he was there, and then I was happy that I hadn't done anything of the sort. At any rate, since I didn't do anything stupid that night, I can now sit here with my head held high. After the initial internal rage, my mind went blank, and it took me a second to collect myself. Then confusion kicked in. *He is here*, I told myself. *He is here; why is he here?*

"Then I heard those magical words. He told me that he was there because he needed somebody to help him, and he had thought of me first. I've always liked it when people feel the need to use my help—even if the person asking for my help was my wife's lover—ex-lover, I mean. I got more excited when he, still standing by the doorstep, told me that he had found the key to immortality, but he couldn't—or rather didn't—want to do it alone and needed the help of someone else, and he had decided to ask me first before asking anyone else. He told me that one of the options he could consider would be to hire someone to help him. I immediately felt so disgusted at the idea of hiring help that I let him in and encouraged him to explain his plan and tell me how he was going to cross the fine border of life and become immortal.

"He told me that he had considered everything; he told me that he wasn't the most famous or successful person in the society, and he couldn't trust his fame to keep his name alive—you know, after he was gone. He told me how concerned he was with the fact that after his normal death, he would be soon forgotten, that no one would even remember his name.

"He told me that for the longest time he had believed that feeling and understanding true love would turn someone immortal in the soul, and such a person would never die. So he had embarked on a futile quest to find true love; eventually, after changing so many lovers, he had discovered that he couldn't find true love. Maybe there was no such thing as true love. Maybe it was all in the stories.

"I found it interesting that he kept talking about true love being a myth. He wouldn't consider the possibility that maybe he just couldn't find the true love of his life; maybe true love actually existed, and he had not known how to look for it and find it.

"In actuality, I agreed with him. I hadn't found true love myself, so I was inclined to accept his reasoning and side with him on that. It is easier for one to accept that true love does not exist than to accept that one has failed to find one's true love. I think it has something to do with one's ego.

"He told me that after feeling the defeat in his quest for true love, he had realized that he needed to find another way to stay alive forever. Staying alive in the mind and soul of every Hay'ati forever seemed unattainable. Everyone dies. He knew that. But immortality and death are not mutually exclusive, he told me. He explained in detail what he wanted me to do and how he was going to achieve immortality. He had thought of everything, and I mean everything—every single detail. It was amazing that what he wanted me to do would not just make him immortal but also it would do the same for me. His plan would make both of us immortal.

"Once he was done explaining, I started to think

about all the details that I had just heard from him. I had a few questions for him, so I started to ask them, especially to make sure that I understood him. My conclusion was that I should help him so that he could achieve his immortality, and I could get my own immortality in the process. Bonus! He had detailed how he wanted me to kill him; it was a horrific and gruesome way. But he wanted me to follow every step. Then I started to ask a few more questions to ensure that he really wanted it. As I said, he had thought of everything. He knew what he wanted. He knew what he wanted me to do, and there was no doubt that he was ready for it. He wanted to make the headlines and stay alive in people's minds and souls for as long as the universe existed. He wanted to be part of our history, to be in the news and books, the subject of many future discussions and deliberations. It seemed like the perfect plan.

"He was my friend, and I wanted to help him reach and achieve his lifelong dream. It was an extra bonus that I could become immortal as well. You know, I didn't feel there was anything in that. I thought I wanted to live as long as he'd live, and that's why I'm sitting here now. He received what he wanted. Now it is my turn; whenever people talk or think about Zula'kier, they will remember my name for as long as the universe exists.

"I'm going to stop talking now; I'm going to need my strength. In a few seconds, that door is going to slide open, and someone will appear, calling my name, and ask me to walk with him. I'm going to need all my strength. I really don't care whether you believed me or not. I don't care if anyone will believe me. I'm just grateful that you listened. I will be the first person ever to have done something like this in Lower Hay'at. I am the first. I am the one."

The old man remained silent.

Part 5

Msa'adam's Last Adventures: The Lion, the Jaguar, and the Wolf

12—Msa'adam's Last Adventures: The Lion, the Jaguar, and the Wolf

Eight hundred thirty-two days after the inception of Lower Hay'at, deep inside the Milky Way galaxy, somewhere on a small green-and-blue planet called Erde, in a marble-made, absolutely silent hallway, stood Msa'adam, alone and scared, his back resting against a stony wall and his front facing the endless, dark hallway. The walls, floor, and ceiling of the hallway were made of black marble; the joints between each square of marble were filled with white and shiny grout. There was a formidable aroma in the hallway. The only sound was Msa'adam's shallow breathing; beads of sweat were on his forehead.

All of a sudden, from afar there came a tapping sound, breaking the silence. The formidable aroma got thicker—so thick that Msa'adam felt he couldn't breathe very well anymore. The tapping sound, which at first was not fully audible, became more and more perceivable. Whatever was causing the sound was slowly getting closer. In the dark the silhouette of an animal soon became visible. An animal was cantering toward Msa'adam with a powerful determination and will. In the darkness, Msa'adam felt the weight of his loneliness and his fear. His breathing became even more shallow and quick. His heart raced, the vein in his neck throbbing.

There was an impenetrable silence again: the animal had stopped moving. The newfound silence was heavy, and it pushed Msa'adam's shoulders down. Despite the painful, heavy, and insufferable silence, Msa'adam felt a sort of soft breeze on his face, something that had not been happening a few minutes before. The breeze smelled as foul as death.

Msa'adam was overcome with desperation; a strong sense of foreboding filled him and made him reach in front of his face. He expected to find the source of the foul-smelling yet gentle breeze. His hands did not touch anything; he felt a deep sense of relief. The silence had become weightless, allowing Msa'adam's shoulders to grow back up.

Msa'adam reached in his pocket. After groping for a moment, he found the lighter he was looking for and took it out. A second later there was enough light in the hallway for Msa'adam to see the most shocking picture of his life: there, a few inches from his face, stood a giant animal. He had never seen an animal as horrifying as this creature. He didn't know the name of the animal, but soon he felt he had sufficient knowledge to recognize the creature. The creature was called a lion. As the knowledge of this creature washed through Msa'adam, he started to learn more about this animal and its desires and feelings. The creature, now quite familiar to Msa'adam, like an old friend, was as tall as Msa'adam was. Its mane was moving gently to his slow breath and the movement of its lungs, and with every heave of its chest, a small cloud billowed from its half-open mouth. There was an unmistakable grin on its face; its brows frowned mischievously. By now Msa'adam knew exactly what the lion wished. He knew very well the deepest desires of any lion.

Msa'adam felt that his heart missed a beat; his brain forgot how to employ his midriff muscles to breathe for a few moments. As the level of oxygen in his bloodstream decreased, a chill that had begun deep down in his stomach started to grow and take over his body, reaching parts as far as his fingers and toes. His body had substituted liquid nitrogen for the missing oxygen. The liquid nitrogen was moving through his veins, causing the veins and everything around them to reach far below zero and freeze fiercely.

Msa'adam expected the lion to charge at any moment now, to attack him, tear him apart, and kill him on the spot. Fear had consumed him thoroughly, and he felt he would die of a heart attack before the lion had time to pounce violently on him to satisfy its savage and primitive hunger.

He dropped the lighter. It made a loud clicking sound as it hit the marble floor, and there was darkness. Msa'adam felt that he could still see the lion. He bent over and reached for his ankles so he did not have to look the lion in the eye when the time came.

It happened more quickly than Msa'adam had expected, and yet to his relief and consternation, nothing happened.

In his mind's eye, he saw the great lion's paw moving up, and he expected the strong claws to shred him into pieces, to drain every ounce of life out of him, and to leave his lifeless body drenched in scarlet blood, but he did not feel anything; nothing happened. He was disappointed that his mental and emotional torture was not over yet and that he would have to wait longer for his painful fate.

Nothing happened...nothing happened; what is more, nothing happened. Still shaking, with shivers running down his spine, little by little, he rose to face his slayer to find out why nothing was happening. Now he was overcome by an overwhelming sense of curiosity. It was dark. He reached for the lighter and picked it up. Standing up straight and tall, he used the lighter, and he saw the fierce lion; its eyes filled with the savage desire to cut its prey into pieces. He saw that the lion was thrashing him with its powerful paws rapidly, but to his amazement, those powerful paws were going through him without making any contact with his flesh or imposing any pain or pressure, mentally or physically, on him. The fierce and irascible lion could not touch him. It was a miracle that those strong paws were just going through him. Msa'adam could see the lion, could feel its breath, and the lion could see, smell, and desire Msa'adam's flesh, and still there was no contact between them.

Msa'adam woke up with a start. His breathing shallow and quick, his face and body drenched in cold sweat, he stared at the ceiling for a moment or two, and then he got up slowly and turned to sit on the edge of the bed, careful not to make any sudden move or sound. He did not want to wake up the pretty woman who was sleeping on the left side of the bed. He turned to look back, in the dark, at the bed and the woman. As he looked at her, the scary and abstruse dream of his perplexing encounter with the creature started to melt away from his memory, leaving its place to the memories of passionate nights he had spent in the very same room on the very same bed—the exhilaration of meeting new partners, glances at each other that would spark amazing attractions, and passionate times they would spend together. Those emotions, however, seemed to belong to a different life or be part of memories of another person. He knew the feelings existed, but all of a sudden, he could not relate to them any longer, as though a thousand years had passed since he had last felt any such emotions. Was he just tired? He moved his gaze up from the woman sleeping, little by little, to the headboard of the bed, where a gorgeously painted jaguar was staring back at him.

A strange sensation overcame him. He had never noticed that painting in his bedroom, and he could not recognize the creature in the painting. Then he started to realize that he knew this animal. He felt this was another carnivore, similar the one he had just seen in his dream.

The jaguar was lying down on a green patch, its spots discernible even in the dark. Its mouth was open in a vague grin or smirk, and its hypnotizing eyes invited and enticed the ignorant victim to move closer and submit willingly to the will of the perfect hunter.

This time, however, the jaguar did not stir any emotions in Msa'adam; he turned away from the bed, got up, crept toward the bedroom door, and left the bedroom quietly. Outside the bedroom, on his way to the kitchen, he stopped in front of a long, rectangular wall mirror and glanced at his stubby, short, and balding reflection. He stared at the lines and hollowed eyes, which were hardly noticeable on his bulky, egg-shaped face. He thought about the things that he had experienced in his life and his previous family, the family that no longer existed. He could remember every little detail of the day that started it all, the day when his son became the chosen one — well, most of the details of that day.

He thought of how he had watched his beloved city grow and how he had nurtured its growth to the point that the city was mature enough to multiply. It was a magnificent success. Once he had reached his immense goal, he had decided to change the direction of his life. Now he had decided to spend the rest of his life living a goalless life — relatively goalless, that is. He wanted power and wanted to maintain the power. But he was tired of leading a life for others; now he wanted to live his life. He wanted his life to choose him. He was no longer interested in reaching deep for any dormant potential he might have or making any attempts to break the bubble surrounding him in order to surmount his uselessness. He was tired of making decisions and fighting.

Many strong fighters experience a point in their lives when they get tired of fighting and decide to let life happen. There are those who never give in, those who continue to fight. But those are rare specimens. Msa'adam had given in long ago. He had achieved all he wanted, and he had gained so much power that he'd never had before. The power kept whispering in his ears that he could do what he wanted, that he could let life happen just as it happens to all powerful people. The power bug had infected him to his core. He had contracted the terminal and incurable power disease. He hadn't known he had the terminal disease until very recently, when it was just too late.

Now, for one incredulous moment, he felt that he had to try again; he had to go back to the front line, fight, and break free, but first he needed some air. He dragged his feet toward the back door in the kitchen, aiming to step into the backyard of his house to get some fresh air. It was past midnight. He could not and did not care what time or what day it was; neither did he care that he would have to wake up in a few hours to go to the meeting with the counselors of Lower Hay'at.

As he got closer to the back door of his house, he felt he could hear some howling noise coming from afar. The closer he got to the door, the louder the howling became. Soon the sound was perceivable enough for Msa'adam to attribute it to a large, dark, and terrifying wolf. Could that really be a wolf? He had seen some wolves when he was younger, but for many years, no one had seen any. He could still remember the sounds of the wolves that he had seen years ago. The howling sound was unmistakably similar to that of a wolf, as he could remember. A few feet from the door, Msa'adam was rooted. He was unable to move his feet any closer to the door. He collected every ounce of his remaining energy, and managed to plough on toward the back door while he felt the source of the howling was definitely in the backyard of his house now.

He was standing in front of the door, the palms of his hands sweaty and resting on the window. His eyes pierced the darkness in search of the source of the horrifying noise that was cutting into the night. His heart was racing; chills were rearing up in the pit of his stomach as something black, terrifying, and heavy jumped at the window, clinging with its black and strong claws to the glass of the window. The mental punch was strong enough to push Msa'adam back a few feet. He fell down and clutched the floor. He was shaking violently, and his face was glistening with large beads of sweat. His chest heaving rapidly, he pulled himself together, brought himself to his hands and knees, and looked up at the window of the back door to see and recognize the frightening monster. There it was: the head of an oversized wolf, two paws, two pointy ears, and in place of two eyes, Msa'adam could see only two empty holes. It seemed that the wolf was standing on its rear legs, propping itself up with its front legs against the window to look at him.

Mustering up all his courage, determination, and will, Msa'adam stood up and strode toward the door to face the wolf. For a moment, Msa'adam felt that he was more curious than scared. He needed to find out why there was a giant and strong wolf at large in the backyard of his home — a wolf, a creature that had been thought to have been extinct many years before.

Listening to the loud howling, Msa'adam reached the back door and glanced through the window to see that the shrubs and cobs of small trees in the backyard were dancing violently to the gusting wind; there was a heavy storm outside, and Msa'adam had not noticed that the howling would be attributable more to the sound of the wind than to a terrifying and alive monster standing by the window of his house.

As Msa'adam was understanding the reason for the noise, there was a loud thud. The angry mouth of the wolf was back by the window. Msa'adam stepped back; this time, however, he smiled at his stupidity as he realized that the wolf was not a wolf at all but a group of branches of the largest tree in the backyard, which he had intended, on so many occasions before, to cut down and never got around to doing.

Msa'adam stepped back, knowing he was no longer going out in the backyard. His change of heart was not due to the stormy and quick-tempered weather, but in fact, as he very well knew deep down, he was afraid that the wolf could be real. He did not want to stand face to face with the carnivore, even though he knew that there was no real animal outside, and it was his imagination that had conjured up the wolf. First the lion and now this wolf? Not to mention the picture in his bedroom that he had never seen before. He felt like having a strong drink to calm him down and clear his mind. His life was built upon his immaculate confidence and unshakable pride, but the question at that moment was whether he should continue living his life the way he was living it. The idea lingered in the air for a second. Msa'adam looked up toward the ceiling as though he wanted to reach out and grab the idea with his hands. He quickly snapped out of it, realizing that real life had been nothing but fighting against first ideas and then people. After the death of his son, he had spent many years showing everyone else the errors of their ways. Once he had succeeded, he had started to spend his life proving to everyone else that he was, in every regard, better and ahead of them. There was no longer any time, not even one second, to waste on theorizing and philosophizing.

Msa'adam turned and walked toward the corner of the kitchen. He opened the basement door and looked at the flight of stairs that led to where he kept his most expensive set of wine bottles. It was very dark, and the end of the stairs was not visible; however, there was a warm and welcoming feeling coming up from the basement. Msa'adam, as he started his descent, thought that he did not need to worry about climbing back up ever again.

Part 6

The Missing Pages of Dr. J. Burgess's Journal

13—The Missing Pages of Dr. J. Burgess's Journal

Day 1144

    The sky must be blue today...difficult to say, though. I have been sitting here all day, thinking about my home and the old life that I had—the life that I left behind. Maybe I did not appreciate what I had.

    Last night was the seventh day in a row that I couldn't get a good night's sleep. With all the horrifying noise, one can hardly get any sleep here. I am tired. I'm very tired. I wish there could be an end to this...to this life...to everything. I can't go back; I don't even know how I could go back. I can't go further either; where would I go? What would be the purpose of moving forward? What is the purpose of anything? I wish I had never left. What is the easiest way to end this? How can I put a stop to my pain? Really, really want this pain to go away...do I have the courage to do it? To end it?

Day 1145

    Another wretched day. Why do I even bother?

Day 1146

    It is such a beautiful day today. Nothing is more rejuvenating than a good night's sleep; I must have read that somewhere. It is the truth. It is amazing how much better I feel now that I have had a couple of nights of good sleep.

    The past few days, with all the weird sounds and the gusts of wind, were petrifying. I think I have learned how to quiet my mind now and just focus on myself. This way, the fear subsides. Time slows down, and I feel I am more in control. I do not want to feel out of control anymore. I am in control of my life. I am in charge.

If someone asked me how I learned to do it, I would say it was necessity. I either had to learn to be in control or go insane. I chose the former. This is how the world should be: I was reading my last journal entry…I don't blame myself for how I felt on that day. Now I am feeling well enough to pack up and move forward…it is a beautiful day today!

Quite some time later…don't know exactly when

I can't remember when it all started…it was a few days after I left my last camp. I was on my way and being as careful as I could. Then everything changed in a flash. I was attacked by some animals. It was fast; I couldn't see what was happening. These animals jumped and came at me from all sides. They tore apart all I had with me; one of them attacked me and bit my arm.

It was very painful. I don't remember much after. I know I fainted. When I came to, it was very cold, and I didn't have much left that I could use. Most of my equipment and package was destroyed. I felt weak (probably because of the blood I had lost). I felt very cold. All I could do was to bandage my wound with what was left. I grabbed some roots to eat. I focused my remaining willpower on finding a place that could keep me safe. I needed a place of refuge.

I found a massive tree with a set of relatively flat branches. This is where I am right now. I feel safer among these branches. I think I slept for a day or two here—it is difficult to say how long. After the attack, I dragged myself out of the world where time was the fourth dimension. Here only three spatial dimensions exist; here time no longer exists.

I have been very weak since the attack. Fortunately, there are a lot of small nests around me…hundreds, actually, and *these small nests are filled with tiny eggs that I just crack open and swallow. I am happy I still have my journal. I feel so alone…so tired. My journal is the only thing helping me get through this ordeal. So weak…so tired. I have no energy left. I think I am going to stay on these branches for a few more days; then I will probably die here. It is at least peaceful here.*

Some more days later

I have been very busy lately. I am feeling a lot better. I can't believe I was thinking I would die. Why do I keep thinking like that?

It has been quite some time since I left my make-believe treehouse. I have been on the road, trying to find food, and have made much progress on my journey. I am now by a river, and I can see this hunk of green trees not far from the riverbank. It is like an island buried under thousands and thousands of trees. I am going to set up camp here and see what I should do next.

Day 1

Since there is no sense of time here, I have difficulty tracking my journal entries, so I have restarted the numbering of my entries.

I have to report that my fever is back.

Day 3

The fever is gone. Now I can focus on the more important things. It is such a relief.

I have decided to find a way to get to the island. I don't feel there is anything else on this road for me to experience or explore, and I can't go back.

Even if I could go back, I would be dealing with the same mundane issues. The island, on the other hand, is waiting to be discovered and explored.

The river is the Amazon's wedding band, and this

massive emerald is the stone. I need to find a way to get to the island.

Day 13

I started the fever again last night. I knew something was going on with me, as I had been sweating for a couple of days.

These jungles have a sharing nature, and they have shared, on many occasions, reasons to experience pain and discomfort. This time is no exception. Right now I have this massive sore throat. I can hardly swallow my saliva, let alone any food. I am feeling very tired, lethargic, and feverish. I will get some rest before I start out again.

Day 26

I am still feeling very tired; my joints are hurting, and I have muscle aches…well, everywhere that I have a muscle. The fever is gone, which is a good sign. I also have a rash all over my body. I don't have enough energy even to write in my journal.

Day 27

The fever is back, and I am constantly feeling nauseous and tired. There is this cough that I cannot shake. When is this going to end?

Day 30

It is a beautiful day, and I am me again! The nausea, rashes, and fever are all gone. I thought for a while that I was not going to make it (well, this is me, always considering the worst!). I am back trying to figure out how I can get to the island. I will start to investigate and try to find a way to get to the island tomorrow.

Day 100

The more I take care of myself, the sicker I get. I have been trying everything, but I feel I am becoming more and more transparent! I know it does not make any sense, but I can hold my hand over a leaf, and I can see the leaf through my hand.

Day 104

I don't have a mirror; I can't see what I look like now. But I can tell that light completely flows through me. I don't leave any footprint when I walk. The truth is that I have started to float. I am convinced this is the island telling me that I don't belong here. I am persistent, though.

I am going to take out the pages that could help someone find the island. I can't have anyone else find it. I will be the only person who knows about this undiscovered island. This island is mine.

I will throw the journal on the river, and hopefully it will survive the torrents, and eventually someone will find it. They will learn about my discoveries. I truly hope my journal finds my son.

I intend to float toward the island. I need to hurry. I can't control my floating. It seems I am floating more and more toward the sky. If I don't hurry, soon I will be floating in the sky over the island.

Even now is too late.

Made in the USA
Las Vegas, NV
23 January 2024

84800223R00069